It was *"Murder, murder most foul..."*

Foster Benedict, his back to the door, was in the chair at the dressing table, half lying among the wigs and make-up boxes.

He was partly dressed in a Don Juan costume. The shirt was of flowing white silk and just below the left shoulder blade, from the apex of a red ragged stain, the handle of a knife protruded . . .

He was a dead Don—
And the cast, the crew, and everyone in
the audience was suspect!

QUEENS FULL

3 Novelets and
A Pair of Short Shorts

Ellery Queen

BALLANTINE BOOKS • NEW YORK

Library of Congress Catalog Card Number: 65-10460

SBN 345-24666-7-150

First Printing: December, 1975

Printed in the United States of America

BALLANTINE BOOKS
A Division of Random House, Inc.
201 East 50th Street, New York, N.Y. 10022
Simultaneously published by
Ballantine Books, Ltd., Toronto, Canada

Contents

The
DEATH
of
DON JUAN

ACT I. Scene 1.

An Early Account of the death of Don Juan Tenorio, fourteenth-century Spanish libertine—who, according to his valet, enjoyed the embraces of no fewer than 2,954 mistresses during his lifetime—relates that the great lover was murdered in a monastery by Franciscan monks enraged by his virility. For four hundred years poets and dramatists have passed up this ending to Don Juan's mighty career as too unimaginative. No such charge can be brought against *their* versions.

Don Juan, they tell us, planted the seeds of his own destruction when he harrowed the virtue of a certain noble young lady, daughter of the commander of Sevilla. While this sort of thing was no novelty to the famous gallant, it was to the young lady; and Don Juan found himself fighting a duel with her father, the commander, whom he killed.

Here the poetic imagination soars. Don Juan visits the tomb of the late victim of his sword. A marble statue of the grandee decorates the tomb. Don Juan invites the

3

statue to a feast, an inexplicable gesture under the circumstances. Having failed in the flesh, the ensculptured nobleman leaps at this second chance to avenge his daughter's ruptured honor. The marble guest shows up at the feast, grasps the roué in his stony clutch, and drags him off to hell. Curtain.

This Don Juan changeling counts among its affectionate foster-parents Molière, Mozart's librettist Da Ponte, Dumas *père,* Balzac, and Shaw. Now to the roster must be added the modest name of Ellery Queen, who has fathered his own. According to Ellery, Don Juan was really murdered in a New England town named Wrightsville, and this is how it came about.

From the days of William S. Hart and Wallace Reid, Wrightsville's dramatic appetite was catered to by the Bijou Theater in High Village. When in the course of human events the movies' fat years turned lean, the Bijou's owner bought up the old scrap-iron dump on Route 478 and on the site built Wright County's first alfresco movie theater, a drive-in that supplanted Pine Grove in the Junction as the favorite smooching place of the young at heart.

This left the two-by-fours nailed over the doors of the abandoned Bijou; and the chairman of the Wrightsville Realty Board, whose office faced the empty building from the other side of Lower Main, vowed at a Board lunch over his fourth old-fashioned that one dark night he was going to sneak over to that eyesore on the fair face of High Village and blow the damn thing up, he was so sick of looking at it.

When, suddenly, Scutney Bluefield bought it.

Scutney Bluefield was a rare specimen in the Wrightsville zoo. Where the young of the first families grew up to work with their money, Scutney played with it. Seven generations of Bluefields had labored and schemed so that Scutney's life might be one grand game. As he often said, his vocation was hobbies. He collected such unexpected things as chastity belts, Minié balls, and shrunken heads. He financed one expedition to prove the historicity of Atlantis and another to unearth the bones of Homer. He flitted from Yoga to Zen to voodoo, and then came back to the Congregational Church. And the old Bluefield mansion on the Hill was usually infested with freeloaders no one in Wrightsville had ever laid eyes on—"my people collection," he called them.

Scutney Bluefield looked like a rabbit about to drop its first litter, but there was a sweet, stubborn innocence in the portly little bachelor that some weedy souls of the region found appealing.

Scutney bought the Bijou because he discovered The Theater. To prepare himself, he lived for two years in New York studying drama, after which he financed a play and watched the professionals spend his money in a lost but educational cause. He hurried home to organize an amateur company.

"No, indeed, no red barns surrounded by hollyhocks for me," he told the Wrightsville *Record* reporter. "My plan is to establish a permanent repertory theater, a year-round project to be staffed by local talent."

"This area hasn't supported professional companies in years, Mr. Bluefield," the reporter said. "What makes you think it will support an amateur one?"

One of the little man's pinkish eyes winked. "You wait and see."

Scutney's secret weapon was Joan Truslow. Joanie was what the boys at the Lions and the Red Men luncheons called "a real stacked little gopher," with natural ash-blond hair and enormous spring-violet eyes. She had been majoring in drama at Merrimac U. when the arthritis got her father and 'Aphas was forced to resign as town clerk. Joan had had to come home and take a job as receptionist at The Eternal Rest Mortuary on Upper Whistling. She was the first to answer Scutney's call, and her audition awed him.

"Wonderful," he had confided to Roger Fowler. "That girl will make us all *proud."*

Rodge was not comforted. A chemical engineer, he had used his cut of Great-Uncle Fowler's pie to buy one of the blackened brick plants standing idle along the Willow River in Low Village and to convert it to Fowler Chemicals, Inc. His interest in Scutney Bluefield's Playhouse was strictly hormonal; he had been chasing Joan Truslow since puberty. To keep an eye on her, young Fowler had offered his services to Scutney, who was not one to look a gift horse under the crupper. The Playhouse needed a technician-in-charge to be responsible for carpentry, props, lights, and other dreary indispensables. So long as the backstage crew functioned, Scutney did not care how many opportunities Roger seized to corner the stage-struck Miss Truslow and, *sotto voce, con amore,* try to sell her a bill of household goods.

Scutney did the Bijou over, inside and out, and renamed it the Playhouse. It cost him a fortune, and of course Emmeline DuPré's was the first voice of doom. (Miss DuPré, known to the cruder element as the Town Crier, taught Dancing and Dramatics to the children of the already *haut monde* of Wrightsville.)

"Scutney will never see a penny of his unearned lucre," Miss DuPré announced.

For once the Town Crier seemed to cry true. The Playhouse was a resounding flop, Joanie Truslow notwithstanding. Scutney tried Shaw, Kaufman and Hart, Tennessee Williams, even (these were conceived in desperation and born calamities) Ionesco and Anouilh; comedy, farce, melodrama, tragedy; the square and the off-beat. They continued to play to dwindling houses.

"Of course, we're not very *good* yet," Scutney reflected aloud after a lethal week.

"Joan's colossal, and you know it," Rodge Fowler said in spite of himself.

"Thank you, sir." Joan's dimple drove him crazy. "I thought you were against careers for females."

"Who's against careers for females? I'm just against a career for you," Roger retorted, hating himself for driving the dimple to cover. "Look, Scutney, how much more of your ancestral dough are you prepared to drop into this cultural outhouse we call home?"

Scutney said in his precise, immovable way, "I am *not* giving up yet, Roger."

A *Record* editorial said: "Is local taste so low that our favorite amusements must be TV Westerns and dramatized deodorant commercials, and movies that give our children the willies? At a time when Wrightsville is reflecting the nationwide jump in juvenile delinquency, alcoholism, dope addiction, gambling, prostitution, and what have you, the community should be supporting Mr. Bluefield's efforts to bring us worth-while dramatic fare. Why not attend the Playhouse regularly, and bring along your teen-agers?"

The empty seats kept spreading like a rash.

A letter to the *Record* signed Cassandra, in a literary style indistinguishable from Emmeline DuPré's, suggested that the Wrightsville Playhouse be renamed the Haunted Playhouse.

When the town's snickers reached the Hill, Scutney's pink eyes turned a murderous red. Very few people in Wrightsville were aware of the paper thinness of Scutney Bluefield's skin.

He flung himself into the Viking throne in his catch-all study, and he thought and he thought.

All at once the name Archer Dullman flew into his head.

Ten minutes later Wrightsville's patron of the performing arts was driving lickety-hop for the airport and the next plane connection to New York.

ACT I. Scene 2.

ELLERY CHECKED IN at the Hollis, showered and changed, cased the lobby, toured the Square (which was round), and returned to the hotel without having seen a single familiar face.

He was waiting for the maître d' (also new to him) in a queue of strangers at the entrance to the main dining room, thinking that time was being its usual unkind self, when a voice behind him said, "Mr. Queen, I presume?"

"Roger!" Ellery wrung young Fowler's hand like Dr. Livingstone at Ujiji. The truth was, he had met Rodge Fowler less than half a dozen times during his various visits to Wrightsville. "How are you? What's happened to this town?"

"I'm fine, and it's still here with certain modifications," Roger said, blowing on his hand. "What brings you this-a-way?"

"I'm bound for the Mahoganies—vacation. I hear you're Wrightsville's latest outbreak of industrial genius."

"That's what they tell me, but who told you?"

"I'm a *Record* mail-subscriber from way back. How come you've joined a drama group, Rodge? I thought you got your kicks in a chem lab."

"Love," Roger said hollowly. "Or whatever they're calling it these days."

"Of course. Joan Truslow. But isn't the company folding? That ought to drop Joanie back into your lap."

Roger looked glum. *"The Death of Don Juan."*

"That old stand of corn? Even Wrightsville—"

"You're not getting the message, man. Starring Mark Manson. Complete with doublet, hose, and codpiece. We open tomorrow night."

"Manson." Ellery stared. "Who dug him up?"

"Scutney Bluefield, via some Times Square undertaker named Archer Dullman. Manson's a pretty lively corpse, Ellery. We're sold out for the run."

"So the old boy still packs them in in Squedunk," Ellery said admiringly. *"Death of Don Juan . . .* This I've got to see."

"There's Scutney at that corner table, with Manson and Dullman. I'm meeting them for supper. Why not join us?"

Ellery had forgotten how much like a happy rabbit Scutney Bluefield looked. "I'm *delighted* you're here for the opening," Scutney cried. "You will be, Ellery, won't you?"

"If I have to hang from a rafter. I haven't had the pleasure of attending one of Mr. Manson's performances in—" Ellery had been about to say "in a great many years," but he changed it to "in some time."

"How are things at the Embassy, Mr. Green?" the actor asked sadly, tilting his cocktail glass, finding it empty, running his forefinger around the inside of the glass, and licking the finger. "You should have seen me with Booth, sir. John Wilkes, that is. Those were the days. *Garçon,* may I trouble you for an encore?" The wavering finger pushed the empty glass into alignment with nine others, whereupon Manson smiled at Ellery and fell asleep. Head thrown back, he resembled a mummy; his gentle, fine-boned face was overlaid with a mesh of wrinkles.

The waitress took their orders. Manson woke up, courteously ordered *Chaud-Froid de Cailles en Belle Vue,* and fell asleep again.

"What's that?" the waitress demanded.

"Never mind, honey. Bring him a rare T-bone."

Scutney looked peevish. "I do hope—"

"Don't worry, Bluefield. He never misses a curtain."

Ellery turned, surprised. The speaker was the man introduced to him as Archer Dullman. He had immediately forgotten Dullman was there. He now saw why. Dullman was not large and not small, neither fat nor thin, ruddy nor pale. Hair, eyes, voice were neutral. It was hard to imagine him excited, angry, amorous, or drunk. Ellery paid close attention to him after that.

"Are you Mr. Manson's manager, Mr. Dullman?"

"It's a buck."

Even so, it was some time before he realized that Dullman had not actually answered his question.

Ellery buttered a roll. "By the way, isn't it an Actors' Equity rule that members may not perform with amateurs?"

It was Scutney who answered; in rather a hurry, Ellery thought. "Oh, but you can almost always get Equity's permission in special cases. Where no Equity company is playing the area, and provided the amateur group initiates the request, deposits the full amount of the member's salary with them, and so forth. Ah, the soup!" He greeted the return of their waitress with relief. "Best chowder in town. Right, Minnie?"

Ellery wondered what was bugging the little man. Then he remembered.

The "Archer" had fooled him. Around Broadway, Dullman was better known as "The Dull Man." It was a typical Broadway quip; Dullman was supposed to be sharper than a columnist's tooth. If Scutney Bluefield had allowed himself to be suckered into a Dullman deal . . .

"They've been calling us the Haunted Playhouse and laughing their heads off," Scutney was chortling. "Who's laughing now?"

"Not me," Rodge Fowler growled. "That scene on the couch between Manson and Joan in the first act is an absolute disgrace."

"How would you expect Don Juan to act on a couch?" Dullman asked with a smile.

"You didn't have to direct it that way, Dullman!"

"Oh, you're directing?" Ellery murmured. But nobody heard him.

"Think of the dear old ladies, Fowler."

"I'm thinking of Joan!"

"Now, Rodge," Scutney said.

Manson chose that moment to wake up. He peered around the crowded dining room and staggered to his feet. His hair-piece had come loose and slipped to one side, exposing a hemisphere of dead-white scalp. He stood there like some aged Caesar in his cups, bowing to his people.

"My dear, dear friends," the actor said; and then, with simple confidence, he slid into Dullman's arms.

Scutney and Roger were half out of their chairs. But Ellery was already supporting the actor's other side.

"Manson can walk, Dullman. Just give him some support."

Between them they dragged Manson, graciously smiling, from the dining room. The lobby seethed with people attending a Ladies' Aid ball; a great many were waiting for the elevators.

"We can't maneuver him through that mob, Dullman. What floor is he on?"

"Second."

"Then let's walk him up. Manson, lift your feet. That's it. You're doing nobly."

Ellery and Dullman hustled him up the staircase toward the mezzanine. Dullman was crooning in the actor's ear, "No more martinis, huh, Mark? So tomorrow night you can step out on that stage in those sexy tights of yours and give these Yokelsville ladies a thrill. You're the great Mark Manson, remember?" Manson made small pleased noises.

Scutney and Roger came running up behind them.

"How is he?" Scutney panted.

"Beginning to feel pain, I think," Ellery said. "How about it, Manson?"

"My dear sir, " the actor said indulgently. "Anyone would think I am intoxicated. Really, this is undignified and unnecessary."

He achieved the mezzanine landing and paused there to recuperate. Ellery glanced at Dullman, and Dullman nodded. They released him. It was a mistake.

Ellery grabbed in vain. *"Catch him!"* But both Scutney and Roger stood there, stunned. Manson, still smiling, toppled backward between them.

Fascinated, they watched the star of *The Death of Don Juan* bounce his way step after step down the long marble staircase until he landed on the lobby floor and lay still.

ACT I. Scene 3.

THEY WENT STRAIGHT from the hospital to Dullman's room at the Hollis. Dullman sat down at the telephone.

"Long distance? New York City. Phil Stone, theatrical agent, West Forty-fourth Street. No, I'll hold on."

"Stone." Scutney was hopping about the room. "I don't know him, Archer."

"So you don't know him," the New Yorker grunted. "Phil? Arch Dullman."

"So what do you want?" Ellery could hear Stone's bass rasp distinctly.

"Philly boy," Dullman said.

"Please, Archie, no routines. It's been an itch of a day, and I was just going home. What's on your mind?"

"Phil, I'm on a spot up here—"

"Up where?"

"Wrightsville. New England."

"Never heard. Can't be a show town. What are you, in a new racket?"

"There's a stock company here just getting started. I made a deal for Mark Manson with this producer to do *Death of Don Juan.*"

"What producer?"

"Scutney Bluefield."

"Whatney Bluefield?"

"Never mind! Opening's tomorrow night. Tonight Manson falls down a staircase in the hotel and breaks the wrist and a couple fingers of his right hand, besides cracking two ribs."

"Old lushes never die. That's all?"

"It's plenty. There might even be concussion. They're keeping him in the hospital twenty-four hours just in case."

"So what?" the agent sounded remote.

"The thing is, they've taped his ribs and put a cast on

his forearm and hand. He won't be able to work for weeks." A drop of perspiration coursed down Dullman's nose and landed on the butt of his cigar. "Phil—how about Foster Benedict?"

Stone's guffaw rattled the telephone.

"Foster Benedict?" Scutney Bluefield looked astounded. He leaped to Dullman's free ear. "You get him, Archer!"

But Ellery was watching Rodge Fowler. At the sound of Benedict's name Roger had gripped the arms of his chair as if a nerve had been jabbed.

Dullman paid no attention to Scutney. "Well, you hyena?"

Stone's voice said dryly, "Might I be so stupid as to ask if this Bluefield and his company are pros?"

Arch Dullman spat his cigar butt, a thing of shining shreds, onto the carpet. "It's an amateur group."

"Look, crook," the agent boomed. "This backwards Sam Harris wants a replacement for Manson, he's got to contact me, not you. He's got to satisfy Equity, not you. You still there, Archie?"

"I'm still here," Dullman sighed. "Here's Bluefield."

Scutney was at the phone in a flash. Dullman picked up the butt and put it back in his mouth. He remained near the phone.

"Scutney Bluefield here," Scutney said nervously. "Do I understand, Mr. Stone, that Foster Benedict is available for a two-week engagement in *The Death of Don Juan*, to start tomorrow night?"

"Mr. Benedict's resting between engagements. I don't know if I could talk him into going right back to work."

"How well does he know the part?"

"Foster's done that turkey so many times he quacks. That's another reason it might not interest him. He's sick of it."

"How much," Scutney asked, not without humor, "will it take to cure him?"

Stone said carelessly, "Fifteen hundred a week might do it."

"Give me that phone!" Dullman said. "Who do you think you're dealing with, Phil? Benedict's washed up in Hollywood, dead on Broadway, and TV's had a bellyful of him. I happen to know he's flat on his tokus. I wouldn't let Mr. Bluefield touch him with a skunk pole if Manson's accident hadn't left us over this barrel. Seven-fifty, Phil, take it or leave it. You taking or leaving?"

After ten seconds the agent said, "I'll call you back." Dullman gave him the number of the Hollis phone and his extension and hung up.

"He'll take." Dullman lay down on the bed and stared at the ceiling.

Scutney began to hop around the room again.

"You're asking for it," Roger Fowler said tightly. "Benedict's a bad actor, Scutney. And I'm not referring to his professional competence."

"*Please*, Roger," the little man said testily. "Don't I have enough on my mind?"

Twelve minutes later the telephone rang. From the bed Dullman said, "You can take it."

"Yes?" Scutney cried.

"We're taking," Stone's bass said. "But you understand, Mr. Bluefield, you got to clear this deal with Equity yourself before we lift a hoof."

"Yes, yes. First thing in the morning."

"I'll be waiting for Equity's go-ahead. Soon as I get it, Benedict's on his way."

"Hold it," Dullman said.

"Hold it," Scutney said.

Dullman got wearily off the bed, whispered something, and returned to the bed.

Scutney pursed his lips. "According to my information, Mr. Stone, Benedict might start out tomorrow for Wrightsville and wind up in a Montreal hotel room with some girl he picked up en route. Can you guarantee delivery?"

"What's that sucker Dullman want, my blood? I'll put him on the plane. That's the best I can do."

Scutney glanced anxiously at Dullman. Dullman shrugged.

"Well, all right, but please impress on Mr. Benedict . . ."

"Yeah, yeah."

"He'll have to change planes in Boston, by the way. There's no through flight. I'll have a car waiting at Wrightsville Airport. If he makes an early enough connection we ought to be able to get in a quick run-through."

"That's up to Equity. Like I said, he ain't moving a muscle—"

"Leave Equity to me. You just get Benedict here."

"Up in his lines," Dullman said.

"Up in his lines," Scutney said, and he hung up. "Archer, that was an inspiration!" Dullman grunted. "Roger, would you run across the Square and ask the *Record* to hold the press? I'll phone them the new copy for tomorrow's ad in a few minutes."

"You're dead set on going ahead with this?" Roger said, not moving.

"Now, Rodge," Scutney said.

Dullman began to snore.

Ellery thought the whole performance extraordinary.

ACT I. Scene 4.

ELLERY MADE HIS way around the Square and into Lower Main under a filthy sky.

It had been an exasperating day for Scutney Bluefield. The little man had been on the long-distance phone to Equity since early morning. By the time the details were straightened out to Equity's satisfaction and Foster Benedict was airborne to Boston, he was on a schedule so tight that he could not hope to set down in Wrightsville before 7:55 P.M. This would give the actor barely enough time to make up, get into costume, and dash onstage for the 8:30 curtain.

Ellery walked into the lobby of the rejuvenated Bijou, pushed through one of the new black-patent leatherette doors, and entered Scutney Bluefield's Playhouse.

The elegantly done-over interior lay under a heavy hush. The cast, made up and in costume, were sitting about the nakedly lit first-act set either sipping coffee containers that might have been poisoned or staring into the gloom of the theater in emotional rapport. A pretty blond girl he recognized as Joan Truslow was stretched out tensely on the set couch where, Ellery surmised, Don Juan Benedict was shortly·to seduce her in the service of art. Roger Fowler, in coveralls, was stroking her temples.

Ellery slipped down the last aisle on his right and through the stage door. He found himself in a cramped triangle of space, the stage to his left. To his right a single door displayed a painted star and a placard hastily lettered MR. BENEDICT. A narrow iron ladder led to a tiny railed landing above and another dressing room.

Curious, Ellery opened the starred door and looked in. Scutney had outdone himself here. Brilliant lighting switched on in the windowless room at the opening of the door. Air-conditioning hummed softly. The driftwood-paneled walls were hung with theatrical prints. Costumes lay thrown about and the handsome tri-mirrored dressing table was a clutter of wigs, hand props, and pots and boxes of theatrical make-up, evidently as Manson had left them before his accident.

Impressed, Ellery backed out. He edged around an open metal chest marked *Tools* and made his way behind the upstage flat to the other side of the theater. Here there was ample space for the property room, the stage entrance, the lighting board, and a spiral of iron steps leading up to half a dozen additional dressing rooms. Beneath them, at stage level, a door announced *Mr. Bluefield. Keep Out.*

Ellery knocked.

Scutney's voice screamed, "I said *nobody!*"

"It's Ellery Queen."

"Oh. Come in."

The office was a little symphony in stainless steel. Scutney sat at his desk, left elbow anchored to blotter, left fist supporting cheek, eyes fixed on telephone. All Ellery could think of was Napoleon after the Battle of Waterloo contemplating what might have been.

Arch Dullman stood at the one window, chewing on a dead cigar. He did not turn around.

Ellery dropped into a chair. "Storm trouble?"

The bunny-nose twitched. "Benedict phoned from the airfield in Boston. All planes grounded."

The window lit up as if an atom bomb had gone off. Dullman jumped back and Scutney shot to his feet. A crash jarred the theatrical photographs on the walls out of alignment. Immediately the heavens opened and the alley below the window became a river.

"This whole damn production is jinxed," Dullman said, glancing at his watch. "They'll be starting to come in soon, Bluefield. We'll have to postpone."

"And give them another chance to laugh at me?" The little Bluefield jaw enlarged. "We're holding that curtain."

"How long do you think we can hold it? Benedict's plane mightn't be able to take off for hours."

"The storm is traveling northwestward, Archer. Boston should be clear any minute. It's only a half-hour flight."

Dullman went out. Ellery heard him order the house lights switched on and the curtain closed. He did not come back.

The phone came to life at 8:25. Scutney pounced on it. "What did I tell you? He's on his way!"

Foster Benedict got to the Playhouse at eighteen minutes past nine. The rain had stopped, but the alley leading to the stage entrance was dotted with puddles and the actor had to hop and sidestep to avoid them. From his scowl, he took the puddles as a personal affront. Scutney and Dullman hopped and sidestepped along with him, both talking at once.

The company waiting expectantly in the stage entrance pressed back as Benedict approached. He strode
past them without a glance, leaving an aroma of whisky
and eau de cologne behind him. If he was drunk, Ellery
could detect no evidence of it.

Rodge Fowler was stern-jawed. And Joan Truslow,
Ellery noticed, looked as if she had just been slapped.

Foster Benedict glanced about. "You—Mr. Bluefish,
is it? Where's my dressing room?"

"At the other side of the stage, Mr. Benedict," Scutney puffed. "But there's no time—"

"They've been sitting out there for over an hour,"
Dullman said. The booing and stamping of the audience
had been audible in the alley.

"Ah." The actor seated himself in the stage door-
man's chair. "The voice of Wrightsburg."

"Wright*ville*," Scutney said. "Mr. Benedict, really—"

"And there, I gather," Benedict said, inspecting the
silent cast, "are the so-called actors in this misbegotten
exercise in theatrical folly?"

"Mr. Benedict," Scutney said again, *"please!"*

Ellery had not seen Benedict for a long time. The
face that had once been called the handsomest in the
American theater looked like overhandled dough. Sacs
bulged under the malicious eyes. The once taut throat
was beginning to string. Only the rich and supple voice
was the same.

"The little lady there," the actor said, his stare settling on Joan. "An orchid in the cabbage patch. What
does she play, Dullman? The heroine, I hope."

"Yes, yes," Dullman said. "But there's no time for introductions or anything, Benedict. You'll have to go on
as you are for the first act—"

"My make-up box, Phil." Benedict extended his arm
and snapped his fingers, his eyes still on Joan. Her face
was chalky. Ellery glanced at Roger's hands. They were
fists.

"Phil Stone isn't here," Dullman said. "Remember?"

"Oh, dear, I forgot my make-up. But does it really matter?"

"There's no time to make up, either! Manson's stuff is still in the star dressing room and you can use his when you dress between acts. Look, are you going on or aren't you?"

"Mr. Benedict." Scutney was trembling. "I give you precisely thirty seconds to get out on that stage and take your position for the curtain. Or I prefer charges to Equity."

The actor rose, smiling. "If I recall the stage business, dear heart, and believe me I do," he said to Joan, "we'll have an enchanting opportunity to become better acquainted during the first act. Then perhaps a little champagne supper after the performance? All *right,* Bluefish!" he said crossly. "Just as I am, eh?" He shrugged. "Well, I've played the idiotic role every other way. It may be amusing at that."

He stalked onstage.

"Places!" Dullman bellowed. Joan drifted away like a ghost in shock. The rest of the cast scurried. "Fowler. Fowler?"

Roger came to life.

"Where's that lights man of yours? Get with it, will you?" As Roger walked away, Dullman froze. "Is that Benedict out there making a *speech?*"

"In the too, too solid flesh," Ellery said with awe, peeping from the wings. Benedict had stepped out on the apron and he was explaining with comical gestures and facial contortions why "this distinguished Wrongsville audience" was about to see the great Foster Benedict perform Act One of *The Death of Don Juan*—"the biggest egg ever laid by a turkey"—in street clothes and *sans* make-up. The audience was beginning to titter and clap.

Ellery turned at a gurgle behind him. Scutney's nose was twitching again.

"What is he *doing?* Who does he think he *is?*"

"Barrymore in *My Dear Children*, I guess." Dullman was chewing away on his cigar. He seemed fascinated.

They could only watch helplessly while Benedict played the buffoon. His exit was a triumph of extemporization. He bowed gravely, assumed a ballet stance, and then, like Nijinsky in *The Spectre of the Rose*, he took off in a mighty leap for the wings.

ACT I. Scene 5.

ELLERY, JAMMED IN with Scutney Bluefield among the standees at the rear of the theater, watched the first act in total disbelief.

Benedict deliberately paraphrased speech after speech. The bewildered amateurs waiting for their cues forgot their lines. Then he would throw the correct cue, winking over the footlights. He capered, struck attitudes, invented business, addressed broad asides to the rocking audience. He transformed the old melodrama into a slapstick farce.

Ellery glanced down at Scutney. What he saw made him murmur hastily, "He's doing far more damage to himself than to you."

But Scutney said, "It's me they're howling at," in pink-eyed fury, and he groped his way through the lobby doors and disappeared.

The seduction scene was an interminable embarrassment. Once during the scene, in sheer self-defense, Joan did something that made Benedict yelp. But he immediately tossed an ad-lib to the audience that Ellery did not catch, and in the ensuing shriek of laughter returned to the attack. At the scene's conclusion Joan stumbled off the stage like a sleepwalker.

Ellery found that he was grinding his teeth.

The curtain came down at last. Ushers opened the fire-exit doors at both sides of the theater. People, wiping their eyes, pushed into the alleys. Ellery wriggled through the lobby to the street and lit a bitter-tasting cigaret. Long after the warning buzzer sounded, he lingered on the sidewalk.

Finally, he went in.

The house lights were still on. Surprised, Ellery glanced at his watch. Probably Benedict needed extra time to get into costume and make up for the second act. Or perhaps—the thought pleased him—Roger had punched him in the nose.

The house lights remained on. The audience began to shuffle, murmur, cough.

Ellery edged through the standees to the extreme left aisle and made for the stage door. It was deathly quiet backstage.

Scutney Bluefield's door was open, and Arch Dullman was stamping up and down the office in a cloud of angry smoke. He seized Ellery.

"Seen Bluefield anywhere?"

"No," Ellery said. "What's wrong?"

"I don't give a damn who Benedict thinks he is," Dullman said. "Even a sucker like Bluefield deserves a better shake. First that moldy hunk of ham turns the first act into a low-comedy vaudeville bit, now he won't answer his call! Queen, do me a favor and get him out of there."

"Why me?"

"I don't trust myself. What's more, you tell him for me that if he doesn't play the rest of this show straight I'll personally bust that balloon he calls a head!"

Ellery's built-in alarm was jangling for all it was worth. "You'd better come with me."

They hurried behind the upstage flat to the other side of the theater. Ellery rapped on the starred door. He rapped again. "Mr. Benedict?"

There was no answer.

"Mr. Benedict, you're holding up the curtain."

Silence.

"Benedict?"

Ellery opened the door.

Foster Benedict, his back to the door, was in the chair at the dressing table, half lying among the wigs and make-up boxes.

He was partly dressed in a Don Juan costume. The shirt was of flowing white silk and just below the left shoulder blade, from the apex of a wet red ragged stain, the handle of a knife protruded.

ACT II. Scene 1.

"THIS CHARACTER IS clean off his chump," Dullman said, jamming a fresh cigar between his teeth. "Imagine playing around with the trick knife and the goo at a time like this. How about acting your age, Benedict? In fact, how about acting?" He brushed past Ellery. "Come on, snap out of it."

"Don't touch him," Ellery said.

Dullman glared at him. "You're kidding."

"No."

Dullman's mouth opened and the cigar fell out. He stooped and fumbled for it.

Ellery leaned over the dressing table, keeping his hands to himself. The skin was a mud-yellow and the lips were already cyanotic. Benedict's eyes were open. As Ellery's face came within their focus they fluttered and rolled.

He saw now that the stain was spreading.

"Bluefield," Dullman said. "My God, where's Blue-field? I've got to find Bluefield."

"Never mind Bluefield. I saw a doctor I know in the audience, Dr. Farnham. Hurry, Dullman."

Dullman turned blindly to the doorway. It was blocked by the cast and the stagehands. None of them appeared to understand what had happened. Joan Truslow had her hand to her mouth childishly, looking at the blood and the knife. As Dullman broke through he collided with Roger Fowler, coming fast.

"What's going on? Where's Joan?"

"Out of my way, damn you." Dullman stumbled toward the stage.

Ellery shut the door and went quickly back to the dressing table. "Benedict, can you talk?"

The lips trembled a little. The jaws opened and closed and opened again, and a thick sound came out. It was just a sound, meaningless.

"Who knifed you?"

The jaws moved again. They were like the jaws of a fish newly yanked from the water. This time not even the thick sound came out.

"Benedict, do you hear me?" The eyes remained fixed. "If you understand what I'm saying, blink."

The eyelids came down and went up.

"Rest a moment. You're going to be all right." You're going to be dead, Ellery thought. Where the devil was Conklin Farnham? He won't be able to touch the knife, he thought.

The door burst open. Dr. Farnham hurried in. Dullman ran in after him and shut the door and leaned against it, breathing hard.

"Hello, Conk," Ellery said. "All I want from him is a name."

Dr. Farnham glanced at the knife wound and his mouth thinned out. He took Benedict's dangling arm without raising it and placed his fingertips on the artery. Then he felt the artery in the temple, examined the staring eyes.

"Call an ambulance."

"And the police," Ellery said.

Arch Dullman opened the door once more. The cast and the stagehands were still standing outside, all except Joan and Roger. Dullman said something to someone and shut the door again.

"Can't you at least stop the bleeding, Conk?"

"It's pretty much stopped by itself."

And Ellery saw that the stain was no longer spreading. "I've got to talk to him. Is it all right?"

The doctor nodded. His lips formed the words *Any minute now.*

"Benedict," Ellery said. "Use the eye signal again. Do you still hear me?"

Benedict blinked.

"Listen. You were sitting here making up. Someone opened your door and crossed the room. You could see who it was in the mirror. Who was it came at you with the knife?"

The bluing lips parted. The tongue fluttered; its sound was like a small bird's wings. Finally a grudging gurgle emerged. Dr. Farnham was feeling for the pulse again.

"He's going, Ellery." This time he said the words aloud.

"You're dying, man," Ellery cried. "Who knifed you?"

The struggle was an admirable thing. He was really trying to communicate. But then over the eyes slipped a substance through which they looked far and away. Without warning the dying man raised his head a full inch from the dressing table, and he held it there quite steadily. He made the fish mouth again.

But from it now, in a confiding whisper, came two words.

Then the head fell back to the table with a noise like wood. The actor seemed to clear his throat. His body stiffened in some last instinctive stubbornness and his breath emptied long and gently and he was altogether empty.

"He's dead," Dr. Farnham said after a moment.

Dullman said in a queer voice, "What did he say?"

"He's dead," Ellery said.

"I mean *him*. I didn't hear what he said from here."

"You heard him, Conk."

"Yes," the doctor said. " 'The heroine.' "

"That's what he said." Ellery turned away. He felt as empty as Benedict looked.

"The heroine." Dullman laughed. "Get what you wanted, Queen? Feel like a big man now?"

"He didn't know her name," Ellery said, as if this explained something important. He was wiping his face over and over.

"I don't understand," Dr. Farnham said.

"Benedict arrived so late tonight there wasn't time for introductions. He could only identify her by her role in the play. The heroine."

Ellery turned away.

"But I took Joan's appendix out when she was fifteen," Dr. Farnham muttered, as if that absolved her. "My father delivered her," as if that clinched it.

Someone rapped on the door. Dullman opened it.

"I'm told something's happened to Mr. Benedict—"

"Well, look who's here," Dullman said. "Come on in, Bluefield."

ACT II. Scene 2.

SCUTNEY BLUEFIELD'S SHOES, the cuffs of his trousers were soaked.

"I've been walking and walking. You see, I couldn't stand what he was doing to the play. I felt that if I stayed one minute longer . . ."

"Scutney," Ellery said.

"And how dreadful," Scutney went on, still looking at the occupied chair. "I mean, he doesn't look human any more, does he? I've never seen this kind of death."

"Scutney—"

"But he brought it on himself, wouldn't you say? You can't go about humiliating people that way. People who've never done you any harm. Who killed him?"

Ellery swung the little man around. "You'll have to talk to your audience, Scutney. I think you'd better use the word accident. And tell your ushers privately not to allow anyone to leave the theater until the police get here."

"Who killed him?"

"Will you do that?"

"Yes, of course," Scutney said. He squished out, leaving a damp trail.

Ellery wandered back to the dressing table. All at once he stooped for a closer look at the knife handle. Dr. Farnham stirred.

"It's a fact they're taking their sweet time," Dullman said. "You want out, Doctor?"

"I left my wife in the audience," Farnham said stiffly.

"Don't worry about Molly, Conk." Ellery dug a small leather case out of his pocket. "And you're my corroborating witness to Benedict's statement."

"That's right," Dullman said. "I didn't hear a thing. I don't have the stomach that goes with ears like yours."

The case produced a powerful little lens, and through it Ellery examined the handle of the knife on both sides.

"What," Dullman jeered, "no deerstalker hat?"

Ellery ignored him. The heavy haft had been recently wound in black plastic friction tape. An eighth of an inch from the edge, the tape showed a straight line of thin, irregular indentations some five-eighths of an inch long. In a corresponding position on the underside there was a line of indentations similar in character and length.

Ellery stowed away his lens. "By the way, Dullman, have you seen this knife before?"

"Any particular reason why I should tell you?"

"Any particular reason why you shouldn't?"

"It's not mine. I don't know whose it is."

"But you have seen it before." When Dullman did not answer, Ellery added, "Believe me, I know how sincerely you wish you were out of this." The way Dullman's glance shifted made Ellery smile faintly. "But you can't wish away Benedict's murder, and in any case you'll have to submit to police questioning. Where have you seen this knife before?"

Dullman said reluctantly, "I don't even know if it's the same one."

"Granted. But where did you see one like it?"

"In that metal tool chest just outside. It was a big-bladed knife with a black-taped handle. From the look of this one I'd say they're the same, but I can't swear to it."

"When did you see it last?"

"I didn't see it 'last,' I saw it once. It was after the first-act curtain. Benedict had weakened one of the legs of the set couch with his damn-fool gymnastics during that scene with the Truslow girl, and even the stage crew was demoralized. So I decided to fix the leg myself. I went for tools, and that's when I spotted the knife. It was lying on the top tray of the chest in plain sight."

"Did you notice any peculiar-looking indentations in the tape?"

"Indentations?"

"Impressions. Come here, Dullman. But don't touch it."

Dullman looked and shook his head. "I didn't see anything like that. I'm sure I'd have noticed. I remember thinking how shiny and new-looking the tape was."

"How soon after the curtain came down was this?"

"Was what?"

"When you saw the knife in the chest."

"Right after. Benedict was just coming offstage. He went into the dressing room here while I was poking around in the tools."

"He was alone?"

"He was alone."

"Did you talk to him?"

Dullman examined the pulpy end of his cigar. "You might say he talked to me."

"What did he say?"

"Why, he explained—with one of those famous stage leers of his—exactly what his plans were for after the performance. Spelled it out," Dullman said, jamming the cigar back in his mouth, "in four-letter words."

"And you said to him—?"

"Nothing. Look, Queen, if I went after every bum and slob I've had to deal with in show business I'd have more notches to my account than Dan'l Boone." Dull-man grinned. "Anyway, you and the doctor here say you heard who Benedict put the finger on. So what the hell."

"Who occupies the dressing room just above this one?"

"Joan Truslow."

Ellery went out.

The lid of the chest marked *Tools* was open, as he had seen it on his backstage tour early in the evening. There was no knife in the tray, or anywhere else in the chest. If Dullman was telling the truth, the knife in Fos-ter Benedict's back almost certainly had come from this tool chest.

Ellery heard two sirens coming on fast outside.

He glanced up at the narrow landing. The upper dressing room door was halfway open.

He sprang to the iron ladder.

ACT II. Scene 3.

HE KNOCKED AND stepped into Joan Truslow's tiny dressing room at once, shutting the door behind him.

Joan and Roger jumped apart. Tears had left a clownish design in the girl's make-up.

Ellery set his back against the door.

"Do you make a habit of barging into ladies' dressing rooms?" Roger said truculently.

"No one seems to approve of me tonight," Ellery complained. "Rodge, there's not much time."

"For what?"

But Joan put her hand on Roger's arm. "How is he, Mr. Queen?"

"Benedict? Oh, he died."

He studied her reaction carefully. It told nothing.

"I'm sorry," she said. "Even though he was beastly."

"I saw his lips moving during your speeches in that couch scene. What was he saying to you, Joan?"

"Vile things. I can't repeat them."

"The police just got here."

She betrayed herself by the manner in which she turned away and sat down at her dressing table to begin repairing her make-up. The trivial routine was like a skillful bit of stage business, in which the effect of naturalness was produced by the most carefully thought-out artifice.

"Anyway, what are people supposed to do, go into mourning?" Roger sounded as if he had been following a separate train of thought. "He was a smutty old man. If ever anyone asked for it, he did."

Ellery kept watching Joan's reflection in the mirror. "You know, Rodge, that's very much like a remark Scutney made a few minutes ago. It rather surprises me. Granted Benedict's outrageous behavior tonight, it was hardly sufficient reason to stick a knife in his back. Wouldn't you say?" The lipstick in Joan's fingers kept flying. "Or—on second thought—does either of you know of a sufficient reason? On the part of anyone?"

"How could we know a thing like that?"

"Speak for yourself, Rodge," Ellery smiled. "How about you, Joan?"

She murmured, "Me?" and shook her head at herself.

"Well." Ellery pushed away from the door. "Oh. Roger, last night in Arch Dullman's room, when Benedict was first mentioned as a substitute for Manson, I got the impression you knew Benedict from somewhere. Was I imagining things?"

"I can't help your impressions."

"Then you never met him before tonight?"

"I knew his smelly reputation."

"That's not what the lawyers call a responsive answer," Ellery said coldly.

Roger glared. "Are you accusing me of Benedict's murder?"

"Are you afraid I may have cause to?"

"You'd better get out of here!"

"Unfortunately, you won't be able to take that attitude with the police."

"Get out!"

Ellery shrugged as part of his own act. He had baited Roger to catch Joan off guard. And he had caught her. She had continued her elaborate toilet at the mirror as if they were discussing the weather. His hostile exchange with Roger should have made her show some sign of alarm, or anxiety, or at least interest.

He left gloomily.

He was not prepared for the police officer he found in charge below, despite a forewarning of long standing. On the retirement of Wrightsville's perennial chief of police, Dakin, the old Yankee had written Ellery about his successor.

"Selectmen brought in this Anselm Newby from Connhaven," Dakin had written, "where he was a police captain with a mighty good record. Newby's young and he's tough and far as I know he's honest and he does know modern police methods. But he's maybe not as smart as he thinks.

"If you ever get to Wrightsville again, Ellery, better steer clear of him. Once told him about you and he gives me a codfish look and says no New York wiseacre is ever going to mix into *his* department. It's a fact there ain't much to like about Anse."

Ellery had visualized Chief of Police Newby as a large man with muscles, a jaw, and a Marine sergeant's voice. Instead, the man in the chief's cap who turned to look him over when he was admitted to the dressing room was short and slight, almost delicately built.

"I was just going to send a man looking for you, Mr. Queen." Chief Newby's quiet voice was another surprise. "Where've you been?"

The quiet voice covered a sting; it was like the swish of a lazily brandished whip. But it was Newby's eyes that brought old Dakin's characterization into focus.

They were of an inorganic blue, unfeeling as mineral.

"Talking to members of the company."

"Like Joan Truslow?"

Ellery thought very quickly. "Joan was one of them, Chief. I didn't mention Benedict's talking before he died, of course. But as long as we had to wait for you—"

"Mr. Queen," Newby said. "Let's understand each other right off. In Wrightsville a police investigation is run by one man. Me."

"To my knowledge it's never been run any other way."

"I've heard tell different."

"You've been misinformed. However, I've known and liked this town and its people for a long time. You can't stop me from keeping my eyes open in their interest and reaching my own conclusions. And broadcasting them, if necessary."

Anselm Newby stared at him. Ellery stared back.

"I've already talked to Dr. Farnham and Mr. Dullman," Newby said suddenly, and Ellery knew he had won a small victory. "You tell me your version."

Ellery gave him an unembroidered account. The police chief listened without comment, interrupting only to acknowledge the arrival of the coroner and issue orders to uniformed men coming in to report. Throughout Ellery's recital Newby kept an eye on a young police technician who had been going over the room for fingerprints and was now taking photographs. Times had certainly changed in Wrightsville.

"Those words Benedict said, you heard them yourself?" the chief asked when Ellery stopped. "This wasn't something Farnham heard and repeated to you?"

"We both heard them. I'm positive Dullman did, too, although he pretended he hadn't."

"Why would he do that?"

Ellery could not resist saying, "You want my *opinion*, Chief?"

The dull blue eyes sparked. But he merely said, "Please."

"Dullman is walking on eggs. This thing is the worst possible break for him. He wants no part of it."

"Why not?"

"Because to admit he heard Benedict's accusation would mean becoming an important witness in an sensational murder case. Dullman can't stand the publicity."

"I thought show people live on publicity."

"Not Dullman. For an Actors' Equity member like Benedict or Manson to work in an amateur company, it has to be a legitimately amateur operation from start to finish. Arch Dullman is an operator. He makes an undercover deal with someone like Scutney Bluefield—desperate to run a successful amateur playhouse—in a setup that otherwise satisfies Equity's strict specifications. Dullman delivers a name-actor—one who's passé in the big time and who'll do anything for eating money —in return for taking over behind the scenes, with Bluefield fronting for him."

"What's Dullman get out of it?"

"He pockets most—or all—of the box-office take," Ellery said. "If this deal with Bluefield became a matter of public record, Dullman might never represent a professional actor again."

"I see." Newby was watching his technician. "Well, that's very interesting, Mr. Queen. Now if you'll excuse me—"

Take that, Ellery thought. Aloud, he said, "Mind if I hang around?"

Newby said politely, "Suit yourself," and turned away.

The knife had been removed from Benedict's back and it was lying on the dressing table. It was a long, hefty hunting knife, its bloodstained blade honed to a wicked edge.

The coroner grunted, "I'm through for now," and opened the door. Two ambulance men came in at his nod and took the body out. "I'll do the post first thing in the morning."

"Could a woman have sunk the knife to the hilt?" Newby asked.

"Far's I can tell without an autopsy, it went into the heart without striking bone. If that's so, a kid could have done it." The coroner left.

Newby walked over to the table. The technician was packing his gear. "Find any prints on the knife?"

"No, sir. It was either handled with a handkerchief or gloves or wiped off afterward. This plastic tape is pretty slick, Chief, anyway."

"What about prints elsewhere?"

"Some of Benedict's on the dressing table and on the make-up stuff, and a lot of someone else's, a man's."

"Those would be Manson's. He used this room all week. No woman's prints?"

"No, sir. But about this knife. There are some queer marks on the handle."

"Marks?" Newby picked up the knife by the tip of the blade and scrutinized the haft. He seemed puzzled.

"There's some on the other side, too."

The chief turned the knife over. "Any notion what made these, Bill?"

"Well, no, sir."

Newby studied the marks again. Without looking around he said, "Mr. Queen, did you happen to notice these marks?"

"Yes," Ellery said.

The chief waited, as if for Ellery to go on. But Ellery did not go on. Newby's ears slowly reddened.

"We could send the knife up to the big lab in Connhaven," the young technician suggested.

"I know that, Bill! But suppose first we try to identify them on our own. Right?"

"Yes, sir."

Newby stalked out to the stage. Meekly, Ellery followed.

The little police chief's interrogation of the company was surgical. In short order he established that between the lowering of the curtain and the discovery of the

dying man, every member of the cast except Joan Truslow had either been in view of someone else or could
otherwise prove an alibi. With equal economy he dis-
posed of the stagehands.

He had long since released the audience. Now he sent
the cast and the crew home.

On the emptying of the theater the curtain had been
raised and the house lights turned off. Scutney Bluefield
and Archer Dullman sat in gloom and silence, too. Each
man an island, Ellery thought; and he wondered how
good an explorer Anselm Newby really was. For the
first time he sensed an impatience, almost an eagerness,
in Newby.

"Well, gentlemen, it's getting late—"

"Chief." Scutney was lying back on the set couch,
thighs and lips parted, gazing up into the flies and managing to resemble an old lady after an exhausting day.
"Are you intending to close me down?"

"No call for that, Mr. Bluefield. We'll just seal off
that dressing room."

"Then I can go ahead with, say, rehearsals?"

"Better figure on day after tomorrow. The Prosecutor's office will be all over the place till then."

Scutney struggled off the couch.

"Oh, one thing before you go, Mr. Bluefield. Did you
see or hear anything tonight that might help us out?"

Scutney said, "I wasn't here," and trudged off the
stage.

"You, Mr. Dullman?"

"I told you all I know, Chief." Dullman shifted the
remains of his cigar to the other side of his mouth. "Is it
all right with you if I go see what's with my client before
somebody does a carving job on him?"

"Just don't leave town. And, Mr. Dullman."

"What?"

"Don't talk about what Benedict said." When Dullman was gone, Newby said, "Well." He got up and
made for the stage steps.

"Chief," Ellery said.

Newby paused.

"You don't have much of a case, you know."

The little policeman trotted down into the orchestra. He selected the aisle seat in the third row center and settled himself. Like a critic, Ellery thought. A critic who's already made up his mind.

"Gotch," Chief Newby called.

"Yes, sir."

"Get Miss Truslow."

ACT II. Scene 4.

JOAN SAILED OUT of the wings chin up, braced. But all she saw was Ellery straddling a chair far upstage, and she began to look around uncertainly.

Roger yelled, "You down there—Newby!" and ran over to the footlights. "What's the idea keeping Miss Truslow a prisoner in her dressing room all this time?"

"Roger," Joan said.

"If you think you've got something on her, spit it out and I'll have a lawyer down here before it hits the floor!"

"Sit down, Miss Truslow," Newby's soft voice said from below. "You, too, Fowler."

Joan sat down immediately.

Whatever it was that Roger glimpsed in her violet eyes, it silenced him. He joined her on the couch, reached for her hand. She withdrew it.

Newby said, "Miss Truslow, when did you make your last stage exit?"

"At the end of my scene with Foster Benedict on the —on this couch."

"How long before the act ended was that?"

"About ten minutes."

"Did you go right to your dressing room?"

"Yes."

"In doing that, you had to pass by the tool chest. Was it open?"

"The chest? I can't say. I didn't notice much of anything." Joan caught her hands in the act of twisting in her lap, and she stilled them. "I was badly upset. They must have told you what he—the way he carried on during our big scene."

"Yes. I hear he gave you a rough time." The little chief sounded sympathetic. "But you did notice the tool chest later, Miss Truslow, didn't you?"

She looked up. "Later?"

"In the intermission. After Benedict got to his dressing room."

Joan blinked into the lights. "But you don't understand, Chief Newby. I went straight to my dressing room and I stayed there. I was . . . frozen, I suppose is the word. I just sat asking myself how I was going to get through the rest of the play. It was all I could think of."

"While you were up there, did you hear anything going on in the room below? Benedict's dressing room?"

"I don't remember hearing anything."

"When *did* you leave your dressing room, Miss Truslow?"

"When I heard all the commotion downstairs. After he was found."

"That was the first time, you say?"

"Yes."

Newby said suddenly, "Fowler, Queen found you with this girl. How come?"

"How come?" Roger snapped. "Why, somebody ran into the prop room to tell me something had happened to Benedict. I ran back with him and spotted Joan in the crowd around Benedict's doorway. I hauled her out of there and up to her dressing room so I could put my arm around her in privacy when she broke down, which she promptly did. Wasn't that sneaky of me?"

"Then that was the first time you saw her after she left the stage?"

"I couldn't get to her before, though God knows I

wanted to. I was too tied up backstage—" Roger halted. "That was sneaky of *you*, Newby. And damn nasty, too! What are you trying to prove, anyway?"

"Miss Truslow, how well did you know Foster Benedict?"

Ellery saw Joan go stiff. "Know him?"

"Were you two acquainted? Ever see him before tonight?"

She said something.

"What? I couldn't hear that."

Joan cleared her throat. "No."

"Logan." A police officer jumped off the apron and darted to his chief. Newby said something behind his hand. The man hurried up the aisle and out of the theater. "Miss Truslow, a witness says that when Benedict went into his dressing room the tool chest was open and a big knife with a taped handle was lying in the tray. I'll ask you again. Did you or didn't you leave your dressing room, climb down, go into the chest—"

"I didn't," Joan cried.

"—go to the chest, pick up the knife—"

"Hold it." Roger was on his feet. "You really want to know about that knife, Newby?"

"You have some information about it?"

"Definitely."

"What?"

"It's mine."

"Oh?" Newby sat waiting.

"I can prove it," Roger said quickly. "If you'll strip the tape off you'll find my initials machine-stamped into the haft. I've used it on hunting trips for years. I brought it to the theater just today. We'd bought some new guy-rope yesterday and I needed a sharp knife—"

"I know all about your ownership of the knife," Newby smiled. "The question isn't who owned the knife, or even who put it in the tool chest. It's who took it out of the chest and used it on Benedict. Miss Truslow—"

"Excuse me," Ellery said. The chief was startled into silence. "Roger, when did you tape the handle?"

"Tonight, after the play started. I'd used it in replacing a frayed guy-rope and I hadn't been able to keep a good grip on it because my hands were sweaty from the heat backstage. So I wound electrician's tape around the haft in case I had to use it again in an emergency during the performance."

"When did you drop it into the chest?"

"Near the end of the act."

"I thought I'd made it clear, Mr. Queen!" The whiplash in the policeman's voice was no longer lazy. "Interrupt once more and out you go."

"Yes, Chief," Ellery murmured. "Sorry, Chief."

Newby was quiet. Then he said, "Now I want to be sure I have this right, Miss Truslow. You claim you went from the stage straight to your dressing room, you stayed there all the time Benedict was being knifed in the room right under yours, you didn't hear a sound, you didn't come down till after Benedict was found dying, and at no time did you touch the knife. Is that it?"

"That's it." Joan jumped up. "No, Roger!" She walked steadily over to the footlights. "Now let me ask you a question, Chief Newby. Why are you treating me as if you've decided I killed Foster Benedict?"

"Didn't you?" Newby asked.

"I did not kill him!"

"Somebody said you did."

Joan peered and blinked through the glare in her eyes. "But that's not possible. It isn't true. I can't imagine anyone making up a story like that about me. Who said it?"

"Benedict, in the presence of witnesses, a few seconds before he died."

Joan said something unintelligible. Newby and Ellery sprang to their feet. But Roger was closest, and he caught her just as her legs gave way.

ACT III. Scene 1.

ELLERY AWOKE AT noon. He leaped for the door and
took in the *Record,* with its familiar yellow label con-
veying the compliments of the Hollis. For the first time
in years the *Record*'s front page ran a two-line banner:

MURDER HITS WRIGHTSVILLE
FAMOUS STAGE STAR SLAIN!

The account of the crime was wordy and inaccurate.
There were publicity photos of Benedict and the cast.
The front page was salted with statements by Dr. Farnham, members of the audience, cast, stage crew, even
police. Chief Anselm Newby's contribution was boxed
but uninformative. The *Record* quoted Scutney Bluefield ("The Playhouse must go on"), Archer Dullman
("No comment"), and Ellery Queen ("Any statement I
might make about Benedict's death would encroach on
the authority of your execellent police chief"). There
was a story on Mark Manson under a one-column cut
showing him at a bar, uninjured arm holding aloft a
cocktail glass ("Mr. Manson was found at the Hollis
bar at a late hour last night on his discharge from
Wrightsville General Hospital, in company of his manager, Archer Dullman. Asked to comment on the tragedy, Mr. Manson said, 'Words truly fail me, sir, which is
why you discover me saying it with martinis.' With the
help of this reporter, Mr. Dullman was finally to per-
suade Mr. Manson to retire to his hotel room").

A choppy review of the first act of *The Death of Don
Juan* showed evidence of hasty editing. What the original copy had said Ellery could only imagine.

The sole reference in print to Joan was a cryptic
"Miss Joan Truslow and Mr. Roger Fowler of the Playhouse staff could not be located for a statement as we
went to press."

Of Foster Benedict's dying words no mention was made.

Ellery ordered breakfast and hurried for his shower. He was finishing his second cup of coffee when the telephone rang. It was Roger.

"Where the devil did you hide Joan last night?"

"In my Aunt Carrie's house." Roger sounded harassed. "She's in Europe, left me a key. Joan was in no condition to face reporters or yak with the likes of Emmeline DuPré. Her father knows where we are, but that's all."

"Didn't you tell Newby?"

"Tell Newby? It's Newby who smuggled us over to Aunt Carrie's. Considerate guy, Newby. He has a cop staked out in the back yard and another in plain clothes parked across the street in an unmarked car."

Ellery said nothing.

"Me, too," Roger said grimly. "I gave Joanie a sleeping pill and stayed up most of the night biting my nails. Far as I know, Newby has no direct evidence against Joan, just those last words of a dying man whose mind was already in outer space. Just the same, I'll feel better with a lawyer around. Before I call one in, though . . ." Roger hesitated. "What I mean is, I'm sorry I blew my stack last night. Would you come over here right away?"

"Where is it?" Ellery chuckled.

Roger gave him an address on State Street, in the oldest residential quarter of town.

It was an immaculately preserved eighteenth-century mansion under the protection of the great elms that were the pride of State Street. The black shades were drawn, and from the street the clapboard house looked shut down. Ellery strolled around to the rear and knocked on the back door, pretending not to notice the policeman lurking inside a latticed summerhouse. Roger admitted him and led the way through a huge kitchen and pantry and along a cool hall to a stately parlor whose furniture was under dust covers.

Joan was waiting in an armchair. She looked tired and withdrawn.

"This is all Roger's idea," she said, managing a smile. "From the way he's been carrying on—"

"Do you want my help, Joan?"

"Well, if Roger's right—"

"I'm afraid he is."

"But it's so stupid, Mr. Queen. Why would Foster Benedict accuse me? And even if he had some mysterious reason, how can anyone believe it? I didn't go near him . . . I've always hated knives," she cried. "I couldn't use a knife on a trout."

"It isn't a trout that was knifed. Joan, look at me."

She raised her head.

"Did you kill Benedict?"

"No! How many times do I have to say it?"

He lit a cigaret while he weighed her anger. She was an actress of talent and resource; her performance the night before in the face of Benedict's coarse horseplay had proved that. It was a difficult decision.

"All right, Rodge," Ellery said suddenly. "Speak your piece."

"It's not mine. It's Joan's."

"I'm all ears, Joan."

Her chest rose. "I lied to Chief Newby when I said I'd never known Foster Benedict before last night. I met Foster six years ago here in Wrightsville. I was still in high school. Roger was home from college for the summer."

"In *Wrightsville?*"

"I know, he acted as if he'd never heard of Wrightsville. But then I realized it wasn't an act at all. He'd simply forgotten, Mr. Queen. He was one of Scutney Bluefield's house guests for a few weeks that summer."

"He didn't even remember Scutney," Roger said bitterly. "Let's face it, the great lover was one step ahead of the butterfly net."

"Then it was a practical lunacy," Ellery remarked. "For six months out of every year in the past ten or

twelve years Benedict practiced house-guesting as a
form of unemployment insurance. Dullman claims he
averaged fourteen, fifteen hosts a year. He must have
had a hard time keeping track. Go on, Joan."

"I was sixteen, and Foster Benedict had been my secret crush for years," Joan said in a low voice. "When I
read the *Record* that he was staying at Mr. Bluefield's
I did a very silly thing. I phoned him."

She flushed. "You can imagine the conversation—
how much I admired his work, my stage ambitions . . .
He must have been having a dull time, because he said
he'd like to meet me. I was in heaven. He began to take
me out. Drives up the lake. Moonlight readings . . . I
certainly asked for it."

She sat forward nervously. "I guess it was like one of
those old-time melodramas—the handsome lecher, the
foolish young girl—the only thing missing was the mort-
gage. Would you believe that when he promised me a
part in his next play I actually fell for it?" Joan laughed.
"And then he went away, and I wrote him some desperate love letters he didn't bother to answer, and I didn't
see or hear from him again until last night.

"And then when he made his royal entrance into the
Playhouse, he not only didn't remember Wrightsville, or
Mr. Bluefield, he'd forgotten me, too." She was staring
into the mirror of the time-polished floor. "I was a
stranger to him. Just another scalp to add to his collection. I'd meant so little to him not even my features had
registered, let alone my name."

"I warned you six years ago Benedict was poison,"
Roger shouted, "but would you listen? Ellery, if you
knew how many times I've begged her to get off this
acting kick and marry me—"

"Let's get to you, Rodge. I take it your evasions last
night covered up a prior acquaintance with Benedict,
too?"

"How could I explain without dragging Joan into it?"

"Then you met him at the same time."

"I knew she was dating him—a high school kid!—

and I'd read of his weakness for the young ones. I was
fit to be tied. I collared him one night after he took Joan
home and I warned him to lay off. I said I'd kill him, or
some such juvenile big talk. He laughed in my face and
I knocked him cold. He was sore as hell about it—I'd
mussed up his precious profile—and he banged right
down to headquarters to prefer charges of assault. That
was when Dakin was chief. But then I guess Benedict
had second thoughts—bad publicity, or something. Anyway, he dropped the charges and left town."

"Did the brawl get into the *Record?*"

Roger shrugged. "It was a one-day wonder."

"And was Joan named in the story?"

"Well, yes. Some oaf at headquarters shot his mouth
off. Dakin fired him."

Ellery shook his head. "You two are beyond belief.
How did you expect to keep a thing like that from Newby?
Last night when you denied having known Benedict,
Joan, didn't you notice Newby send one of his men on
an errand? He's a city-trained policeman—he wouldn't
take your word. He'd check the *Record* morgue and his
own headquarters files. He may even have phoned the
New York City police to search Benedict's apartment—
Benedict's bragged often enough in print about his col-
lection of feminine love letters.

"So Newby either knows already, or he'll very soon
learn, that you lied to him on a crucial question, and exactly what happened six years ago, and exactly why.
Don't you see what you've handed him on a silver platter?"

Joan was mute.

"From Newby's viewpoint there's a strong circumstantial case against you, Joan. Situated in the only other dressing room on that side of the theater, you had the
best opportunity to kill Benedict without being seen.
The weapon? You wouldn't have had to move a step out
of your way en route to Benedict's dressing room to take
the knife from the tool chest. What's been holding Newby up is motive."

Joan's lips moved, but nothing came out.

"Newby knows perfectly well that Benedict's conduct onstage last night, rotten as it was, toward a girl who'd never laid eyes on him before would hardly pass muster as a reason for her to run for the nearest knife. But with the background of that romance between you six years ago in this very town, Joan, and your lie about it, and especially if the New York police dig up your letters, Benedict's humiliation of you in public last night takes on an entirely different meaning. It becomes a motive that would convince anybody.

"Add to opportunity, weapon, and motive Benedict's dying declaration, and you see how near you are to being formally charged with the murder."

"You're a help," Roger stormed. "I thought you'd be on Joan's side."

"And on yours, Roger?"

"Mine?"

"Don't you know you're Newby's ace in the hole? You threatened six years ago to kill Benedict—"

"Are you serious? That was just talk!"

"—and you beat him up. You've admitted the knife that killed Benedict is yours, and you brought it to the theater the day of the murder. You probably can't account for your whereabouts during every minute of the short murder period. If not for Benedict's statement, Newby would have a stronger case against you than against Joan. As it is, Rodge, you may be facing an accessory charge."

For once Roger found nothing to say. Joan's hand stole into his.

"However," Ellery said briskly. "Joan, do you still maintain you didn't kill Benedict?"

"Of course. Because I didn't."

"Would you be willing to take a test that might prove you didn't?"

"You mean a lie detector test?"

"Something far more direct. On the other hand, I've got to point out that if you did kill Benedict, this test might constitute evidence against you as damning as a fingerprint."

Joan rose. "What do I do, Mr. Queen?"

"Rodge, ask the police officer in the car parked across the street to drive Joan and you to Newby's office. I'll meet you there." He took Joan's hand in both of his. "This is beginning to shape up as quite a girl."

"Never mind her shape," Roger said. "Can't you go with us?"

"I have something to pick up first," Ellery said, "at a hardware store."

ACT III. Scene 2.

HE WALKED INTO Anselm Newby's office with a small package under his arm to find Joan and Roger seated close together under Newby's mineral eye. A tall, thin man in a business suit turned from the window as Ellery came in.

"Fowler's been telling me about some test or other you want to make, Queen," the little police chief said acidly. "I thought we'd agreed you were to keep your nose out of this case."

"That was a unilateral agreement, you'll recall," Ellery said, smiling. "However, I'm sure you wouldn't want to make a false arrest, and the Prosecutor of Wright County wouldn't want to try a hopeless case. Isn't that so, Mr. Odham?" he asked the man at the window.

"So you know who I am." The tall man came forward with a grin.

"The *Record* runs your photo with flattering regularity."

Prosecutor Odham pumped Ellery's hand. "Art Chalanski, my predecessor, has told me some fantastic stories about you."

"Apparently Chief Newby doesn't share your enthusiasm for fantasy," Ellery murmured. "By the way, Mr. Odham, you *were* about to charge Joan Truslow with the Benedict murder, weren't you? I haven't dared ask the chief."

Newby glared and Prosecutor Odham chuckled. But there was no humor in his frosty gray eyes.

"What have you got, Mr. Queen?"

Ellery said politely to the police chief, "May I see the knife?"

"What for?"

"In a moment. Don't worry, Chief. I shan't so much as breathe on it."

Newby opened the safe behind his desk and brought out a shallow box padded with surgical cotton. The blood-stained knife lay on the cotton. He held on to the box pointedly.

"This thin short line of indentations in the tape of the handle." Ellery made no attempt to touch the knife. "Have you determined yet what made them, Chief?"

"Why?"

"Because they may either blow up your case against Joan or nail it down."

Newby flushed. "You'll have to show me."

"I intend to. But you haven't answered my question. Have you decided what kind of marks these are?"

"I suppose you know!"

"Anse," Odham said. "No, Mr. Queen, we haven't. I take it you have?"

"Yes."

"Well?" Newby said. "What are they marks of?"

"Teeth."

"Teeth?" The Prosecutor looked startled. So did Joan and Roger.

"Maybe they're teeth marks and maybe they're not," Newby said slowly, "though I admit we didn't think of teeth. But even if they are. Only two could be involved—"

"Four," Ellery said. "Two upper and two lower— there are corresponding impressions of the other side of the haft. What's more, I'm positive they're the front teeth."

"Suppose they are. These could only be edge impressions, and they're certainly not distintive enough for a positive identification."

"You may be right," Ellery said soberly. "They may not prove to be positive evidence. But they may well prove to be negative evidence."

"What's that supposed to mean?"

"Suppose I can demonstrate that Joan Truslow's front teeth couldn't possibly have left these marks? Or any pairs of her contiguous upper and lower, for that matter? Mind you, I don't know whether they demonstrate any such thing. The only teeth I've experimented with so far are my own. I've explained to Joan the risk she's running. Nevertheless, she's agreed to the test."

"Is that so, Miss Truslow?" the Prosecutor demanded.

Joan nodded. She had a death grip on the sides of her chair seat. As for Roger, he had entangled himself in an impossible combination of arms and legs, like a barricade.

Odham said, "Then, Mr. Queen, you go right ahead."

Ellery's package remained intact. "Before I do, let's be sure we agree on the significance of the teeth marks. Last night Roger told us he didn't put the freshly taped knife in the tool chest backstage until the act was nearly over. Rodge, were those marks in the tape when you dropped the knife in the chest?"

"You've forgotten," Roger said shortly. "I've never seen them."

"My error. Take a look."

Roger untangled himself and took a look. "I don't see how they could have been. The knife wasn't out of my possession until I put it in the chest, and I'm certainly not in the habit of gnawing on knife handles." He went back to Joan's side and barricaded her again.

"What would you expect Fowler to say?" Newby said.

Joan's hand checked Roger just in time.

"Well, if you won't accept Roger's testimony," Ellery said, "consider Arch Dullman's. Dullman last night said he saw the knife in the chest directly after the curtain came down—as Benedict came off stage, in fact—and he was positive there were no indentations in the tape at that time. Didn't Dullman tell you that, Chief?"

Newby bit his lip.

"By the testimony, then, someone bit into the tape after Benedict entered his dressing room and before we found him. In other words, during the murder period." Ellery began to unwrap his package. "The one person who we know beyond dispute handled the knife during the murder period was the murderer. It's a reasonable conclusion that the impressions were made by the murderer's teeth."

Chief Newby's teeth were locked. But Odham said, "Go on, Mr. Queen, go on."

Out of the wrappings Ellery took a roll of new black plastic friction tape and a large hunting knife. He stripped the cellophane from the roll and handed roll and knife to Roger. "You taped the original knife, Rodge. Do a repeat on this one." Roger set to work. "Meanwhile, Joan, I'd like you to take a close look at the original."

Joan got up and walked over to Newby. She seemed calmer than the chief.

She really has talent, Ellery thought. "Notice the exact position of the marks relative to the edge of the handle."

"About an eighth of an inch from the edge."

"Yes. Oh, thanks." Ellery took the test knife from Roger and gave it to Joan. "I want you to take two bites. First with your front teeth about an eighth of an inch from the edge, as in the other one." He looked at her. "Go ahead, Joan."

But Joan stood painfully still.

"The moment of truth, Joan?" Ellery said with a smile. "Then try the Method. You're a pirate and you're boarding the fat Spanish galleon with a knife in your teeth, like any self-respecting buccaneer." He said sharply, "Do it."

Joan breathed in, placed the haft to her mouth, and bit into it firmly. Ellery took it from her at once and examined the marks. "Good! Now I want you to take a second bite—well clear of the first, Joan, so the two don't overlap. This time, though, make it a full bite."

When she returned the knife Ellery ran to the window. "May I have the other one, Chief?" He was already studying the test impressions through his lens. Newby, quite pale, brought the murder weapon, Odham at his heels.

Joan and Roger remained where they were, in a dreadful quiet.

"See for yourselves."

The police chief peered, squinted, compared. He went back to his desk for a transparent ruler. He made a great many deliberate measurements. When he was through examining the upper surfaces of the hafts he turned the knives over and did it all again.

Finally he looked up. "I guess, Mr. Odham," he said in a rather hollow voice, "you'd best check these yourself."

The Prosecutor seized the knives and lens. Afterward, there was a glint of anger in his eyes. "No impressions of any two adjoining teeth, either in the matching bite or the full set, are identical with the impressions on the murder knife. Same sort of marks, all right, but entirely different in detail—not as wide, not the same spacing —there can't be any doubt about it. You have a lot to thank Mr. Queen for, Miss Truslow. And so do we, Anse. I'll be talking to you later."

Not until Odham was gone did Joan's defenses crumble. She sank into Roger's arms, sobbing.

Ellery turned to the window, waiting for Newby's explosion. To his surprise nothing happened, and he turned back. There was the slender little chief, slumped on his tail, feet on desk, looking human.

"I sure had it coming, Queen," he said ruefully. "What gripes me most is having put all my eggs in one basket. Boom."

Ellery grinned. "I've laid my quota of omelets. Do you know anyone in this business who hasn't?"

Newby got to his feet. "Well, now what? Between Benedict's putting the finger on this girl and your removing it, I'm worse off than when I started. Can you make any sense out of this, Queen?"

"To a certain point."

"What point's that?"

Ellery tucked his lens away. "I know now who did the job on Benedict and why, if that's any help."

"Thanks, buddy."

"No, I mean it."

"I wish I could appreciate the rib," Newby sighed, "but somehow I'm not in the mood."

"But it's not a rib, Chief. The only thing is, I haven't a particle of proof." Ellery rubbed his nose as Newby gaped. "Though there *is* a notion stirring . . . and if it should work . . ."

ACT III. Scene 3.

The Following Morning's *Record* shouted:

LOCAL GIRL CLEARED IN KILLING!

The lead story was earmarked "Exclusive" and began:

Joan Truslow of the Wrightsville Playhouse company was proved innocent yesterday of the Foster Benedict murder by Ellery Queen, the *Record* learned last night from an unusually reliable source.

Miss Truslow, allegedly Chief Anselm Newby's main suspect in the Broadway star's sensational killing, was cleared by the New York detective in a dramatic session at police headquarters. A secret demonstration took place in the presence of Chief Newby and Prosecutor Loren Odham of Wright County. The exact nature of the test was not disclosed, but it is said to have involved the knife that slew Benedict.

Chief Newby would neither affirm nor deny the *Record*'s information.

"I will say that Miss Truslow is not a suspect," Newby told the *Record*. "However, we are not satisfied with some of her testimony. She will be questioned further soon."

Asked whether he was referring to strong rumors around headquarters last night, Chief Newby admitted that Miss Truslow is believed to be withholding testimony vital to the solution of the murder.

By press time last night Miss Truslow had not been located by newsmen. She is said to be hiding out somewhere in town.

Prosecutor Odham could not be reached, *etc.*

The *Record* story's "Exclusive" tag was an understandable brag. Wire service and metropolitan newspaper reporters had invaded Wrightsville at the first flash of Foster Benedict's slaying, and the war for news raged through the town. The *Record* disclosure almost wrecked Scutney Bluefield's plans to take up his personal war with Wrightsville's Philistines where mere murder had broken it off.

Scutney had sent out a call for his entire company. They converged on the Playhouse the morning the *Record* story broke to find the forces of the press drawn up in battle array. In a moment the surrounded locals were under full-scale attack; and Scutney, purple from shouting, sent to police headquarters for reinforcements.

A wild fifteen minutes later Chief Newby laid down the terms of a truce.

"You people have one hour out here for interviews with Mr. Bluefield's company," the chief snapped. "Nobody gets into the theater after that without a signed pass from me."

As it turned out, the newsmen retired from the field in less than half their allotted time. One of their two chief objectives was not present: Ellery had slipped out of the Hollis early in the morning and disappeared.

Their other target, Joan, who showed up at the Playhouse with Roger, had refused to parley. To every question fired at her about "the testimony vital to the solution" she was reported to be withholding, Joan looked more frightened and shook her head violently. "I have nothing to say, nothing," she kept repeating. Nor would she reveal where she was staying. On being attacked in his turn, Roger became totally deaf. In the end, he had charged into the theater with her, and the press beat a disgusted retreat shortly after, to bivouac at various High Village bars.

Chief Newby stationed police at the stage entrance, fire exits, and in the lobby, and left for an undisclosed destination.

So it was with slightly hysterical laughter that the company greeted Scutney Bluefield's opening words: "Alone at last."

They were assembled onstage under the working lights. Scutney had hopped up on a set chair.

"You'll all be happy to hear that we're going right ahead with *The Death of Don Juan.*" He raised his little paw for silence. "With due respect to the late Foster Benedict, he saw fit to make a farcical joke out of our production. We're going to do it *properly.*"

Someone called out, "But, Mr. Bluefield, we don't have a Don Juan."

Scutney showed his teeth. "Ah, but we will have, and a good one, too. I shan't disclose his name because I haven't completed the business arrangements. He should be joining us the day after tomorrow.

"I spent most of yesterday making cuts and line changes and revising some of the business, especially in Act One, where I think we've been in danger of wrong audience reactions. Today and tomorrow we'll go over the changes, so we ought to be in good shape when our new Don Juan gets here. Meanwhile, as a favor to me, Mr. Manson has kindly consented to walk through the part for us. Does anyone need a pencil—?"

They plunged into the work with relief.

The day passed quickly. Sandwiches and coffee were brought in twice. There was only one interruption, when a tabloid photographer tried to get into the theater by stretching a ladder across the alley between a window in the next building and the Playhouse roof. But he was intercepted, and an extra policeman was assigned to the roof.

It was almost ten o'clock when Scutney called a halt. The company began to disperse.

"Not you, Miss Truslow!"

Joan stopped in her tracks. It was Chief Newby.

"I haven't wanted to interfere with Mr. Bluefield's working day. But now, Miss Truslow, you and I are going to have a real old-fashioned heart-to-heart talk. Whether it takes five minutes or all night is up to you. I think you know what I'm talking about."

Joan groped for one of the set chairs. "I have nothing to tell you! Why won't you let me alone?"

"She's out on her feet, Chief," Roger protested. "Can't this wait?"

"Not any more," Newby said quietly. "You stay where you are, Miss Truslow, while I get rid of those newspapermen outside. I don't want the papers in on this just yet. I'll come back for you when the street's clear."

The theater emptied. Lights began winking out. One harsh spotlight remained onstage. Joan cowered in its glare.

"Roger, what am I going to do? I don't know what to do."

"You know what to do, Joanie," Roger said gently.

"He won't let go of me till . . ."

"Till what? Till you tell him what you're hiding?" Roger pushed a curl of damp blond hair back from her forehead. "I know you've been hiding something, darling. I've known it longer than Newby. What is it? Can't you tell even me?"

Joan's hands quivered in her lap.

"He's bound to get it out of you tonight."

"Rodge—I'm afraid."

"That's why I want you to share it with me, baby. Look, Joan, I love you. What good would I be if I didn't share your troubles?"

"Rodge . . ."

"Tell me."

She swallowed twice, hard, looking around nervously. The deep silence of the theater seemed to reassure her.

"All right. All right, Rodge . . . The other night—during the intermission—when I was in my dressing room feeling so hurt by Foster's not remembering me . . ."

"Yes?"

"I decided to go down to his dressing room and—and . . . Oh, Rodge, I don't know why I wanted to! Maybe to tell him what I thought of him . . ."

"Hurry it up," Roger urged her. "The reason doesn't matter! What happened?"

"I was about to step onto the ladder from the landing when I heard Foster's dressing-room door open below, and . . . *I saw him.*"

"The murderer?" Roger cried.

Joan nodded, shuddering. "I saw him sneak out . . . and away."

"Did you recognize him?"

"Yes."

"But my God, Joan, why didn't you tell Newby?"

"Because he'd accuse me of making it up. At that time the chief was sure I'd done it."

"But now he knows you didn't!"

"Now I'm just plain scared, Roger."

"That Benedict's killer will come after you? He's not getting the chance!" Roger cupped her chin fiercely. "You're ending this nightmare right now, young lady. Let me get out of these work clothes, and then you're going outside to tell Newby who murdered Benedict—and the more reporters hear it the better. Don't move from here, Joanie. I'm only going as far as the prop room—I'll be right back!"

The darkness swallowed him. His rapid footsteps died away.

Joan found herself alone on the stage.

She was perched stiff-backed on the edge of the big Spanish chair at the base of the light cone formed by the spot. There was no other lights anywhere. The dark surrounded and held her fast, like walls.

The dark and the silence. The silence that had reassured her before now made her uneasy.

Joan began to move her head. They were small, jerky movements. She kept probing here and there with furtive glances, over her shoulder, toward the invisible wings, out into the blackness crouching beyond the dead footlights.

"Rodge?" she called.

The quaver of her own voice only brought the silence closer.

"*Roger?*"

Joan curled up in the chair suddenly, shut her eyes tight.

And as if drawn to the place of her imprisonment by her fear, a bulky blob of something detached itself from the murky upstage formlessness and crept toward the light.

It began to take stealthy shape.

The shape of a man.

Of a man with something gripped at chest level.

A knife.

"*Now!*" Ellery's roar dropped from the catwalk far over the stage like a bomb.

Quick as Chief Newby and his men were, Roger was quicker. He hurtled out of the wings and launched himself at the man with the knife like a swimmer at the start of a race. He hit the man at the knees and the man went over with a crash that rattled the stage. The knife went skittering off somewhere. The man kicked out viciously, and Roger fell on him and there was a sickening *crack!* and the man screamed, once. Then he was still.

As soon as he could, Chief Newby hurried to the set

chair. "That was as good an act as Broadway ever saw! And it took real guts, Miss Truslow." He bent over the chair, puzzled. "Miss Truslow?"

But Miss Truslow was no longer acting. Miss Truslow had peacefully passed out.

ACT III. Scene 4.

ONE OF THE waitresses in the Hollis private dining room was clearing the table as the other poured their coffee.

"I hope you didn't mind my choice of menu, Joan," Ellery was saying.

Under the cloth her fingers were interwoven with Roger's. "How could I mind such a lovely steak?"

"I was commemorating the steak knife he lifted from the Hollis in your honor."

"In case I forgot?" Joan laughed. "That was the longest dream of my life, Ellery. But I'm awake now, and that's even lovelier."

"Queen, where's the dessert you promised?" Chief Newby asked. "I've got a lot to do at headquarters."

"No dessert for me," Joan said dreamily.

"Likewise," Roger said likewise.

"You don't eat this dessert," the chief explained, "you listen to it. Anyway, *I'm* listening."

"Well, it goes like this," Ellery began. "I kept urging Benedict, as he was dying, to tell me who stabbed him. When he was able to get some words out, seconds before he died, Conk Farnham and I were sure we heard him say, 'The heroine,' an unmistakable accusation of you, Joan. You were heroine of the play, and Benedict didn't know—or, as it turned out, didn't remember— your name.

"But then the tooth-mark test proved Joan's innocence. Dying men may accuse innocent persons falsely in mystery stories, but in life they show a deplorably simple respect for the truth. So Benedict couldn't have meant the heroine of the play. He must have meant a word that sounded like heroine but meant something else. There's only one word that sounds like heroine-with-an-e, and that's heroin-without-an-e.

"The fact was," Ellery continued, "at the very last, Benedict wasn't answering my who-did-it question at all. His dying mind had rambled off to another element of the crime. Heroin. The narcotic."

He emptied his coffee cup, and Chief Newby hastily refilled it.

"But no dope was found," Joan protested. "Where could dope have come into it?"

"Just what I asked myself. To answer it called for reconstructing the situation.

"When the act ended, Benedict entered the star dressing room for the first time. He had forgotten to bring along his make-up kit and Arch Dullman had told him to use the make-up in the dressing room. In view of Benedict's dying statement, it was now clear that he must have opened one of the boxes, perhaps labeled make-up powder, and instead of finding powder in it he found heroin."

"Benedict's finding of the dope just pointed to the killer," Newby objected. "You claimed to be dead certain."

"I was. I had another line to him that tied him to the killing hand and foot," Ellery said. "Thusly:

"The killer obviously didn't get to the dressing room until Benedict was already there—if he'd been able to beat Benedict to the room no murder would have been necessary. He'd simply have taken the heroin and walked out.

"So now I had him standing outside the dressing room, with Benedict inside exploring the unfamiliar make-up materials, one box of which contained the heroin.

"Let's take a good look at this killer. He's in a panic. He has to shut Benedict's mouth about the dope before, as it were, Benedict can open it. And there's the tool chest a step or two from the door, the tape-handled knife lying temptingly in the tray.

"Killer therefore grabs knife.

"Now he has the knife clutched in one hot little hand. All he has to do is open the dressing-room door with the other—"

"Which he can't do!" Newby exclaimed.

"Exactly. The haft of the knife showed his teeth marks—he had held the knife in his mouth. A man with two normal hands who must grip a knife in one and open a door with the other has no need to put the knife in his mouth. Plainly, then, he didn't have the use of both hands. One must have been incapacitated.

"And that could mean only Mark Manson, one of whose hands was in a cast that extended to the elbow."

Joan made a face. "Really, Roger, was it necessary to break his wrist all over again last night?"

"I didn't like where he'd aimed that kick." Roger grinned at her and she yanked her hand away, blushing. He promptly recaptured it.

"Don't mind these two," Newby said. "You sure make it sound easy, Queen!"

"I shouldn't have explained," Ellery sighed. "Well, the rest followed easily, at any rate. The night before, the hospital said they would keep Manson under observation for twenty-four hours. So he must have been discharged too late on opening night to get to the theater before the play started. He must have arrived during intermission.

"With the audience in the alleys and the fire-exit doors open, all Manson had to do was drape his jacket over his injured arm to conceal the cast, mingle with the crowd in the alley, stroll into the theater, and make his way to the backstage door on the side where the star dressing room is. He simply wasn't noticed then or afterward, when he slipped out and parked in the Hollis bar —where Dullman and the *Record* reporter found him."

"But Mark Manson and *dope*," Joan said.

Ellery shrugged. "Manson's an old man, Joan, with

no theatrical future except an actors' home and his scrapbooks. But he's still traveling in stock, hitting small towns and big-city suburbs. It's made the perfect cover for a narcotics distributor. No glory, but loot galore."

"He did a keen Wrightsville business before he took that tumble. We've already picked up the two local pushers he supplied." Chief Newby folded his napkin grimly. "Middlemen in the dope racket are usually too scared to talk, but I guess the pain of that wrist you broke for him all over again, Fowler, was kind of frazzling. Or maybe he figures it'll help when he comes up on the murder rap. Anyway, Manson got real chatty last night. The Feds are pulling in the big fish now."

Ellery pushed his chair back. "And that, dear hearts, as the late Mr. Benedict might have said, is my cue to go on. On to that vacation waiting for me in the Mahoganies."

"And for yours truly it's back to work," Newby said, following suit.

"Wait! Please?" Joan was tugging at Roger's sleeve. "Rodge . . . haven't you always said——?"

"Yes?" Roger said alertly.

"I mean, who wants to be an actress?"

That was how it came about that young Roger Fowler was seen streaking across the Square that afternoon with young Joan Truslow in breathless tow, taking the short cut to the town clerk's office, while far behind puffed the chief of police and the visiting Mr. Queen, their two witnesses required by law.

E=MURDER

THE TITLE OF Ellery's lecture being The Misadventures of Ellery Queen, it was inevitable that one of the talks on his tour should be crowned by the greatest misadventure of all. It came to pass just after his stint at Bethesda University, in the neighborhood of Washington, D.C., where misadventures of all sorts are commonplace.

Ellery had scribbled the last autograph across the last coed's Humanities I notebook when the nearly empty auditorium resounded with a shout, almost a scream.

"Mr. Queen, wait! Don't go yet!"

The chancellors of great universities do not ordinarily charge down center aisles with blooded cheeks, uttering whoops and Ellery felt the prickle of one of his infamous premonitions.

"Something wrong, Dr. Dunwoody?"

"Yes! I mean probably! I mean I don't know!" the head of Bethesda U. panted. "The President . . . Pentagon . . . General Carter . . . Dr. Agon doesn't— Oh, hell, Mr. Queen, come with me!"

Hurrying across the campus in the mild Maryland evening by Dr. Dunwoody's heaving side, Ellery managed to untangle the chancellorial verbiage. General Amos Carter, an old friend of Ellery's, had enlisted the services of Dr. Herbert Agon of Bethesda University, one of the world's leading physicists, in a top-secret experimental project for the Pentagon. The President of the United States himself received nightly reports from Dr. Agon by direct wire between the White House and the physicist's working quarters at the top of The Tower, Bethesda U.'s science citadel.

Tonight, at the routine hour, Dr. Agon had failed to telephone the President. The President had then called Agon, and Agon's phone had rung unanswered. A call to the Agon residence had elicited the information from the physicist's wife that, as far as she knew, her husband was working as usual in his laboratory in The Tower.

"That's when the President phoned General Carter," Dr. Dunwoody wailed. "It happens that the General was closeted with me in my office—a, well, a personal matter—and that's where the President reached him. When General Carter heard that you were on campus, Mr. Queen, he asked me to fetch you. He's gone on ahead to The Tower."

Ellery accelerated. If Dr. Agon's experiments involved the President of the United States and General Amos Carter, any threat to the safety of the physicist would, like the shot fired by the rude bridge that arched the flood, echo round the world.

He found the entrance to the ten-story aluminum-and-glass Tower defended by a phalanx of campus police. But the lobby was occupied by three people: General Amos Carter; a harassed-looking stalwart in uniform, the special guard on Tower night duty; and a young woman of exceptional architecture whose pretty face was waxen and lifeless.

"But my husband," the young woman was saying, like a machine—a machine with a Continental accent. "You have no right, General. I must see my husband."

"Sorry, Mrs. Agon," General Carter said. "Oh, El-lery—"

"What's happened to Dr. Agon, General?"

"I found him dead. Murdered."

"Murdered?" The crimson in Chancellor Dunwoody's cheeks turned to ashes. "Pola. Pola, how dreadful."

General Carter stood like a wall. "It's dreadful in more ways than one, Doctor. All Agon's notes on his experiments have been stolen. Ellery, for the next few minutes I can use your advice."

"Of course, General. First, though, if I may . . . Mrs. Agon, I understand from Dr. Dunwoody that you're a scientist in your own right, a laboratory technician in Bethesda's physics department. Were you assisting your husband in his experiments?"

"I know nothing of them," Pola Agon's mechanical voice said. "I was a refugee, and although I am now a naturalized citizen and have security clearance, it is not for such high-priority work as Herbert was doing."

Dr. Dunwoody patted the young widow's hand and she promptly burst into unscientific tears. The chancel-lor's arm sneaked about her. Ellery's brows went aloft. Then, abruptly, he turned to General Carter and the guard.

The top floor of The Tower, he learned, consisted of two rooms: the laboratory and the private office that housed Dr. Agon's secret project for the Pentagon. It was accessible by only one route, a self-service, nonstop elevator from the lobby.

"I suppose no one may use this elevator without iden-tification and permission, Guard?"

"That's right, sir. My orders are to sign all visitors bound for the top floor in and out of this visitors' book. There's another book, just like it, in Dr. Agon's office, as a further check." The guard's voice lowered. "There was only one visitor tonight, sir. Take a look."

Ellery took the ledger. He counted twenty-three en-tries for the week. The last name—the only one dated

and timed as of that evening—was James G. Dunwoody.

"You saw Dr. Agon tonight, Doctor?"

"Yes, Mr. Queen." The chancellor was perspiring. "It
had nothing to do with his work, I assure you. I was
with him only a few minutes. I left him alive—"

The General snapped, "Guard?" and the guard at
once stepped over to block the lobby exit, feeling for his
holster. "You go on up to Agon's office, Ellery, and see
what it tells you—it's all right, I've locked the laboratory door." The General turned his grim glance on the
head of Bethesda University and the murdered man's
widow. "I'll be up in a minute."

General Carter stepped out of the elevator and said,
"Well, Ellery?"

Ellery straightened up from the physicist's office desk.
He had found Agon's body seated at the desk and
slumped forward, a steel letter-knife sticking out of his
back. The office was a shambles.

"Look at this, General."

"Where'd you find *that?*"

"In Agon's right fist, crumpled into a ball."

Ellery had smoothed it out. It was a small square
memorandum slip, in the center of which something had
been written in pencil. It looked like a script letter of the
alphabet:

"E," General Carter said. "What the devil's that supposed to mean?"

Ellery's glance lifted. "Then it isn't a symbol connected with the project, General—code letter, anything like
that?"

"No. You mean to tell me Agon wrote this before he died?"

"Apparently the stab wasn't immediately fatal, although Agon's killer might have thought it was. Agon must have revived, or played dead, until his killer left, and then, calling on his remaining strength, penciled this symbol. If it has no special meaning for you, General, then we're confronted with a dying message in the classic tradition—Agon's left a clue to his murderer's identity."

The General grunted at such outlandish notions. "Why couldn't he have just written the name?"

"The classic objection. The classic reply to which is that he was afraid his killer might come back, notice it, and destroy it," Ellery said unhappily, "which I'll admit has never really satisfied me." He was scowling at the symbol in great puzzlement.

General Carter fell back on orderly facts. "All I know is, only one person came up here tonight, and that was Dunwoody. I happen to know that Dunwoody's in love with Pola Agon. In fact, they had a blowup about it at the Agons' house last night—Agon himself told me about it, and that's why I was in Dunwoody's office this evening. I don't give a damn about these people's private lives, but Agon was important to the United States, and I couldn't have him upset. Dunwoody admits he lost his temper when Agon accused him of making a play for Mrs. Agon—called Agon a lot of nasty names. But he claims he cooled down overnight, and came up here tonight to apologize to Agon.

"For my money," the General went on grimly, "Dunwoody came up here tonight to kill Agon. It's my hunch that this Pola Agon is a cleverly planted enemy agent, out after Agon's experimental notes. She's played Mata Hari to Dunwoody—she's sexy enough!—and got him to do her dirty work. It wouldn't be the first time an old fool's turned traitor because of his hormones! But we'll find those notes—they haven't had time to get them away. Ellery, you listening?"

"E," Ellery said.

"What?"

"E," Ellery repeated. "It doesn't fit with the name James G. Dunwoody—or with Pola Agon, for that matter. Could it refer to Einstein's $E = mc^2$, where E stands for energy . . . ?" He broke off suddenly. "Well, well! Maybe it isn't an E after all, General!"

He had moved the memorandum slip a quarter-turn clockwise. What General Carter now saw was:

"But turned that way it's an M!" the General exclaimed. "Who's M? There's no initial M in this, either." He eyed the dead physicist's phone nervously. "Look, Ellery, thanks and all that, but I can't sit on this much longer. I've got to notify the President . . ."

"Wait," Ellery murmured. He had given the memo slip another quarter-turn clockwise.

"Now it's a 3!"

"Does 3 mean anything to you or the project, General?"

"No more than the others."

"Visitor number 3 . . . ? Let me see that check-in book of his." Ellery seized the duplicate visitors' book on the dead man's desk. "Agon's third visitor this week was . . ."

"Who?" General Carter rasped. "I'll have him picked up right away!"

"It was you, General," Ellery said. "Of course, I assume—"

"Of course," the General said, reddening. "Now what the deuce are you doing?"

Ellery was giving the memo sheet still another clockwise quarter-turn. And now, astonishingly, it read:

"W?"

"No," Ellery said slowly. "I don't think it's a W . . . General, wasn't Agon of Greek extraction?"

"So what?"

"So Agon might well have intended this to stand for the Greek letter omega. The omega looks very like an English small script *w*."

"Omega. The end." The General snorted. "This was certainly Agon's end. Poetry yet!"

"I doubt if a scientist *in extremis* would be likely to think in poetic terms. Numbers would be more in character. And omega is the last letter of the twenty-four-letter Greek alphabet. Number twenty-four, General. Doesn't something strike you?"

General Carter threw up his hands. "No! What?"

"Twenty-four's proximity to the number of visitors Agon actually received up here this week—which was twenty-three, you'll recall, Dr. Dunwoody tonight being the twenty-third. Surely that suggests that Agon meant to indicate *a twenty-fourth visitor*—someone who came after Dunwoody? And if that's true, Agon's killer was his twenty-fourth visitor. That's what Agon was trying to tell us!"

"It doesn't tell me a thing."

"It tells us why Agon didn't write his killer's name or initials. He denoted his visitor by number, not because he was afraid the killer might return and destroy the clue—a pretty far-fetched thought process for a man nine-tenths dead!—but because *he simply didn't know his murderer's name.*"

General Carter's eyes narrowed. "But that would mean it was someone Agon knew only by sight!"

"Exactly," Ellery said. "And if you'll do a security re-check on the skunk, General, you'll find it's his loyalty to the United States, not Mrs. Agon's or Dunwoody's, that's been subverted."

"*What* skunk?" the General bellowed.

"The only skunk who could have got up here without signing in. That worried-looking night guard on duty in the lobby."

The

WRIGHTSVILLE

HEIRS

I

WHEN SAMUEL R. LIVINGSTON died, his three children buried him in Twin Hill Cemetery, patted their stepmother hastily, and took off for civilization. There was nothing to hold them in Wrightsville, not even their mother's grave. The first Mrs. Livingston, a Back Bay expatriate, had specified burial in Boston. "I was buried in Wrightsville," her will explained, "long enough."

The second Mrs. Livingston, nee Bella Bluefield, had grown up next door to Sam Livingston, and what she had felt when he went to Boston for a wife she never told anyone. But when the mother of Sam's children died, Bella was still next door waiting. He made her their stepmother as soon as he decently could.

"You should have been their mother, Bella," Sam said.

"I will be, Sam."

But she never was. Samuel Junior, Everett, and Olivia came home from their private schools and their jaunts about Europe to peck at her cheek, make polite inquiries about her health, commend her currant pie, and then they went away again and forgot her existence. They treated her from the first with affectionate amusement, as if she were a quaint old family retainer.

After their father's death, aside from a rare well-bred note from Samuel Junior, an occasional jocular postcard from Everett, or another wedding announcement from Olivia, they dropped out of Bella Livingston's life.

So she grew old alone, trying to fill the gaps with the committee meetings and organizational luncheons so dear to the hearts of old ladies everywhere. Then when she suffered that purely frightful attack and Dr. Conklin Farnham began warning her that her heart was no longer reliable, Bella took Amy Upham to live with her.

Amy hailed from the lower end of Hill Drive, where the shade trees were tallest and the houses predated the Revolution. An orphan, she had been brought up by her widower-uncle, Dr. Horace Upham, whose practice among the poor of Low Village was the largest and least "paying" in Wrightsville. Then Dr. Upham himself sickened, and during his long last illness Amy abandoned her pre-med course at Merrimac U. to nurse him. Her uncle died leaving nothing but uncollectible bills; the old house was sold for debts, and Amy found herself without home or means of any but menial support. That was when Bella Livingston offered her a paid companion's job. Amy leaped at it.

Amy was naturally cheerful, and she bustled about the Livingston mansion leaving order and sunshine in her wake. Dorcas Bondy and Morris Hunker, the "staff," soon came to adore her. As old Dorcas sniffed to her mistress, "What did we ever do around here without that lamb?"—a question Bella Livingston had been asking herself with increasing frequency.

Sometimes the old lady was troubled. "I feel so guilty, Amy. This is no life for a young girl, especially one as pretty as you. Being buried in this draughty old museum."

"Buried!" Amy would laugh. "I love it—and you."

And old Bella would kiss her, knowing it was true. She had watched Amy Upham grow up—much like herself—needing someone who needed her. They never talked about the boy Amy had been engaged to, the one who was killed in Viet Nam; or about Amy's parents, whom she could not remember.

But the old lady talked often about her stepchildren, whose careers she kept following in the Wrightsville *Record* with firm interest. As the Livingston file in the *Record*'s morgue grew, Bella's grimness grew with it.

So Amy was surprised one day when the old lady suddenly said, "Amy, get in touch with Samuel Junior, Everett, and Olivia and tell them—wherever they are— to come see me."

"But will they?" Amy exclaimed.

"They will if you say I want them to. They're too well-bred to refuse. Breeding," said Bella dryly, "is my stepchildren's long suit."

They arrived on a weekend in early summer.

At first Amy thought them charming. Olivia was like an expensive jewel, exquisitely cut and set, and unbreakable; but there were humanizing puffs of fatigue under her quite lovely eyes, her clothes were wonderful, and she greeted Amy with no trace of the condescension Amy had half expected. Everett proved a jovial sort, broad and stocky, with a skin like an overbaked potato; he engulfed her hand and said tenderly how touched they all were for the way she was taking care of "Mother." And Samuel Junior, the eldest, seemed a darling—a tall thin stooped man with a courtly manner who might have stepped out of a John P. Marquand novel.

The old lady was waiting serenely for them on the front lawn when Morris Hunker chauffeured them up from Wrightsville Airport in the old Livingston Lincoln, and she personally directed Morris's disposition of their luggage.

"You've given us our old bedrooms, Bella," Olivia said, when they rejoined her on the lawn. "How sweet."

"It was sweet of you all to come," said the old lady

sweetly. "Amy dear, have Dorcas fetch the tea."

When Amy returned with Dorcas and the tea wagon, she found them conversing amiably.

"I never could see that fellow, Sis," Samuel Junior was drawling. "He wore hand-painted neckties."

"Which husband was that, Olivia?" the old lady asked with interest. "The Prussian baron or the Hungarian count?"

"The Spanish prince," said Olivia, wrinkling her nose.

"The one who cost you two hundred thousand dollars?"

"Oh, dear," said Olivia. "No sugar, thank you, Amy. *Lots* of lemon."

"With your figure?" Amy smiled. "Look what Dorcas's cooking is doing to mine."

"I haven't stopped looking since I got here," said Everett Livingston. "Warm day, isn't it? How about a swim, Amy?"

"Don't," Olivia said to Amy.

"Traitor." Her brother scowled. "Why, Bella, GaGa's on the market again. She's between husbands, you know."

"GaGa?" said the old lady. "Oh, yes, your newspaper name."

"So it finally got to Wrightsville," said Olivia calmly.

"Death to journalism," said Everett, raising his teacup. "When is the cocktail hour, Bella?"

"Later," Bella Livingston said, and smiled. "And by the way, the newspapers haven't treated you very nicely, either, Everett, have they? I've often wondered why you thought you could make money out of sports."

"An all-American nomination and that million from Father. Oh, well. Cheers."

"Let's see," the old lady ruminated. "Your professional football team, that midget auto-racing venture . . . both of those failed, didn't they? And now I read you're trying to buy into a professional basketball team."

"Lovely girl you have here, Bella," said Everett. "Lovely."

"Thank you, Mr. Livingston," Amy murmured.

"Ev. No, really, Amy, let's cool off in the pond."

"Don't," Olivia said to Amy again.

"And you, Samuel," said the old lady, setting her tea-cup down. "You lost yours in oil and mines, didn't you? The latest, I hear, is uranium."

"Was," said Samuel Junior, reaching for a peanut-butter sandwich. "Was, Bella. Yes, you find us all finan-cially mortified, which I take it is the point of all this."

"In fact," said Everett, but looking at Amy, "broke."

"Of course, in my case there's always dear old Charles," said Olivia. "My Texas oil admirer, Bella. But Charles has such filthy table manners."

"Marry him anyway, GaGa," her brother Everett urged. "If he'd finance that basketball deal I'd cut him in for forty-five percent. And maybe five for little you."

"Don't be vulgar, Ev."

"Don't be stupid, Ev," said Samuel Junior. "Charlie Waggoner sold me the wells I dropped a quarter of a million in."

There was a lull. The old lady kept smiling at them. Amy began to feel uncomfortable.

"All right, Bella dear." Samuel Junior smiled back. "You've had your best fears confirmed. Why the sum-mons?"

"I'll tell you after supper, Samuel. Herbert Wentworth's coming."

"Father's old legal beagle?"

"Old Mr. Wentworth's been dead for years. His son took over the management of the estate."

"That'll be real jolly," said Everett Livingston. "Amy, at least let's walk down to the pond for a *look*. I'll show you where I once almost drowned GaGa."

"Show *me*," said Olivia grimly, rising. "Excuse us?"

Samuel Junior wandered off after them.

When the three had disappeared, Amy said quietly, "Aren't you overexciting yourself, Mother Livingston?"

"You do know me, dear, don't you?" The old lady's cheeks were bright pink. "By the way, Olivia is taking care of Everett, I'm glad to see, so don't worry."

"As long as I stay out of a bikini I imagine I'm safe," said Amy, smiling. "You're sure you're all right?"

"Just fine, dear."

But Amy fretted about her all through supper. Olivia chattered about Cannes and the international set, a rather sulky Everett diagrammed the blood lines of a racing thoroughbred he was thinking of buying, and Samuel Junior gallantly commended the currant pie, while the old lady's pinkness deepened.

Herbert Wentworth arrived on the tick of eight. He was a cadaverous Yankee with a voice like a water-logged harp.

There was no mistaking where Mr. Wentworth's sympathies lay. "I'll go over this with no hems and no haws," he announced frigidly when they were all settled in the vast crypt of the drawing room. "Under the terms of Samuel R. Livingston's will, each of his three children was left one million dollars, supposedly aggregating the bulk of his fortune. The widow was left the real and personal property plus the residuary estate. This was believed at the time to be just enough to take care of Mrs. Livingston's needs.

"However." Mr. Wentworth surveyed the prodigals without joy. "A secret codicil to your father's will enjoined my father, as administrator of the estate, from disclosing the true state of affairs to you; and your stepmother was directed to keep it a secret from you, too."

"Why?" demanded Everett.

His sister said softly, "Shut up, *darling*."

"Because," retorted the lawyer with a smack of his dentures, "your father was worth a whole lot more than he let on, and he didn't want you to know it till you became responsible enough to handle it. Samuel Livingston didn't think his children had the proper respect for capital."

"So"—and they all turned at the sound of her voice

to stare at Bella Livingston—"your father left it up to me to decide when—if ever—you were to get it. Herbert, read the codicil."

Mr. Wentworth took a rather worn document from his briefcase and read it through in a resounding twang. Then he handed it to Samuel Junior. Samuel Junior read it and passed it to his brother. Everett read it and tossed it to his sister. Olivia studied it for some time before she handed it back to the lawyer.

"The codicil doesn't mention figures," Olivia said brightly. "How much does it amount to, Bella?"

The old lady glanced at her, and Olivia flushed.

"For a long time I thought Sam was wrong to deprive you of the extra money just because of me. So years ago I made a will leaving everything to you three in equal shares. But"—and at the word the trio grew very still—"now I know that Sam's fears about you were justified. Give me one good reason why I should leave the money to you."

"The best reason in the world, Bella," Olivia said reasonably. "The money was Father's and we're his children."

"The money is mine, and how have you ever treated me? Any of you?"

There was a silence. Amy began to wish she could get out of the room without being noticed.

"Why, very decently, I've always thought—" began Everett in a hearty tone.

"Everett, what date is my birthday?"

Everett glanced swiftly at Olivia, who just as swiftly turned to her elder brother.

"Don't look at me, *I* don't know, either," said Samuel Junior. "You're perfectly right, old dear, we've been absolute swine. But, Bella," her eldest stepchild asked ruefully, "who else is there to leave it to?"

"Amy."

Amy almost fell off the arm of the old lady's chair. The waxy hand reached up to touch her.

"Since your father was taken from me, this child has

been the only soul in the world who's cared if I lived or died. She's run my house, fed me, read to me, managed my card parties, rubbed my feet, cheered me up, nursed me through a heart attack. She's devoted her young life to keeping me comfortable and happy, for no reward but the salary I pay her. I couldn't love Amy Upham more if she were my own.

"But you three *are* my husband's children," Bella Livingston went on with some difficulty, "and it's been very hard knowing the right thing to do. That's why I had to see you again. I know Dr. Farnham doesn't think my heart will survive another attack. I've got to make a decision one way or the other, and do it soon."

The stout old body struggled to rise. Amy helped her, hardly knowing what she was doing.

"I've given myself till Sunday to decide about a new will," said the old lady; and she went out leaning on Amy's arm.

That was a Friday evening.

At seven-thirty Sunday morning Amy, still in her bathrobe, trudged upstairs from the kitchen with the old lady's "wake-up" coffee, entered the master bedroom with a cheerful *"Good* morning!" and found Bella Livingston glaring back at her from the huge curly-maple bed, dead.

On Tuesday morning next, the shrilling of his telephone roused one Ellery Queen from his sleep in his Manhattan apartment, and a twanging voice identified the caller as one Attorney Herbert Wentworth of Wrightsville. Mr. Wentworth, it appeared, was sorry to be phoning so early but it was at the urgent suggestion of Mr. Queen's friend Chief of Police Dakin, and could Mr. Queen catch the next plane for Boston and the Wrightsville connecting plane? Old Mrs. Bella Livingston had died Sunday and Chief Dakin was sure now it was murder, and a real baffler at that.

"At first, Mr. Queen," said Chief Dakin, looking more like a sorrowing Abe Lincoln than ever, "Amy thought old Bella had died of a heart attack. But something about the look of things made her phone Mr. Wentworth and me without waking up the three Livingstons. On Coroner Grupp's and the lab's reports I'm satisfied now that one of those three snuck into the old lady's bedroom in the middle of the night of Saturday–Sunday, around three A.M., and held a pillow over her face till she smothered to death. The thing is, which one? Nothing to tell that I can see, and I've questioned 'em and studied reports till I'm blue in the face."

"Murder." Mr. Wentworth sounded soggy.

Ellery looked the room and the reports over for the fourth time. Dakin had driven him from the airport to the mansion on the Hill, saying that with everyone over at Willis Stone's Eternal Rest Mortuary on Upper Whistling, where the services were going on, they would have the Livingston place to themselves.

The emptiness of the big old house had weight.

"I see nothing here, Dakin," Ellery said at last. "Let's go downstairs and talk."

The silence was less oppressive in the drawing room.

"Now, Mr. Wentworth, about the old lady's visit to your office."

"There were two visits, Mr. Queen. The first was a week ago Monday, four days before those three got to town. Morris Hunker drove her to High Village—"

"Alone?"

"Yes. She'd come in, she said, to ask me what the right wording of a holograph will would be 'in case' she wanted to write one. I gave her a sample will form, told her it wasn't a smart idea for anybody to try and write her own will, she just thanked me politely, and left."

"What about her second visit?"

"That was Saturday—morning after the conference here, when she told 'em they were her heirs but she was thinking of changing the will. She used the excuse of a D.A.R. lunch in High Village to come down to my office in a taxi without anyone knowing, not even Amy. She brought with her a new will she told me she'd written out late Friday night—a will, she said, that nobody knew about yet."

"Decided not to wait for Sunday after all." Ellery nodded. He looked grim. "She must have decided that urgency was the order of the day. What does her new will provide, Mr. Wentworth?"

"Don't know. It was on a single sheet, folded so only the space for the signatures showed. My law clerk and my office girl witnessed her signature, she sealed the envelope herself in our presence, and she waited till I locked it up in my office safe."

"Somebody's in for a real shock." Chief Dakin glanced at his watch. "They're about ready to bury old Bella now."

Ellery rose. "Let's get out to the cemetery."

He was puzzled, and he thought the funeral might tell him something.

The Livingston plot on the sunny west slope of Twin Hill Cemetery smelled of breeze, grass, and grief. All the tottering Hill contingent were there, Bella Livingston's lifelong friends—Hermione Wright, the Granjon clan, the Wheelers, the Minikins, Judge Eli Martin, Emmeline DuPré, and the rest; Amy Upham, her pretty face swollen, stricken, and lost; old Dorcas weeping and Morris Hunker honking his nose; and Bella Livingston's three stepchildren tightly knotted, but with no false show of sorrow. Ellery thought it clever of them.

He watched them closely as Dr. Doolittle lowered his Book and the silent scattering began. But the three merely made the slow correct march back to the Lincoln and there waited patiently for Amy.

And back at the house on the Hill they were unreadable, too. Chief Dakin introduced Ellery with calculated brutality as "come up from New York to look into Bella's murder." Amy clung to Mr. Wentworth as if he were her one remaining tether to the past, seeming hardly to realize why Ellery was there. But the Livingstons chatted with him charmingly; and when the lawyer produced a long envelope sealed with red wax and, clearing

his throat, asked everyone to be seated, they nested
'own side by side in the dead old lady's slip-covered
sofa with martinis in their hands and just the right air of
well-bred expectancy.

They remained that way while Wentworth broke the
seal and opened the envelope and took out a sheet of
white onionskin paper . . . while he unfolded it and
held it up to the sunlight coming in through the bay window so that line after line of closely spaced handwriting
showed through. Only when he read the date did their
sad smiles stiffen.

" 'I, Bella Bluefield Livingston, residing at 410 Hill
Drive, Wrightsville,' " Mr. Wentworth's damp twang in-
formed them, " 'do hereby make, publish, and declare
this to be my last will and testament, *revoking all other
and former wills and codicils heretofore made by
me . . .' "

So there was the ending before the story was well begun.

Everett's shrug was a masterwork: *That is definitely
that,* it said. *Nice going, girl,* was the message of Olivia's
smile to Amy Upham. And Samuel Junior stared into
his empty cocktail glass and its obvious symbolism like
the gentleman-philosopher he appeared to be.

And yet to one of them, Ellery mused, it must be a
sickening blow. There was something to be said for the
discipline of breeding, at that.

He went over to follow the shaky but determined
handwriting on the paper in Wentworth's hands as a
cover for his surveillance. Provision for funeral expen-
ses, payments of debts and taxes, the Wentworth law
firm as administrator, bequests to Dorcas Bondy, Morris
Hunker, and several Wrightsville charities . . . Then:

" 'The property on Hill Drive, both real and personal,
and the income from the residue of my estate—the principal value of which totals about $1,000,000—I leave to
my dear young friend and companion Amy Upham, for
the duration of her lifetime. On Amy Upham's death the
principal estate is to pass to my late husband's three

children, Samuel Junior, Everett, and Olivia, in equal shares; or in the event of the predecease of any or all of them, to his or their heirs or assigns.' "

Ellery could only admire them. In a body they rose and went to Amy, struck dumb in her chair, and congratulated her as sportsmen gracefully acknowledge a race well run but lost.

"Well, gentlemen," said Samuel Junior, turning to them, "that would seem to settle that."

"Yes," said Ellery, "but not the question of who smothered Bella Livingston three nights ago."

They looked pained.

"Am I to understand from that remark, Mr. Queen," asked the tall elder brother courteously, "that one of us is seriously suspected of having murdered our stepmother?"

"Can you offer another suggestion, Mr. Livingston?"

"That's not my province. Though I should think a tramp—"

"Tramps break into houses to steal, Mr. Livingston. There was no break-in, and nothing was stolen or even disturbed. No convenient sneak thief, I'm afraid."

"Then may I point out that Olivia, my brother, and I gain nothing at all by our stepmother's death?"

"Murder is not wiped off the books," Ellery reminded Samuel Livingston, Junior, with matching courtesy, "on the ground that it fails to show a profit. The facts indicate that no one involved knew your stepmother had executed a new will Saturday morning. If that's so, she was murdered Saturday night by someone who thought the old will was still in force. By someone, you see, who *would* have gained. And that's a perfectly valid motive."

"And that's us." Olivia laughed. "Forgive me, darlings. I'm trying to see myself smothering Bella."

"The trouble with you fellows is," said Everett, "you have the typical middle-class attitude about money. It's really not that important."

"The whole notion is mad." Samuel Junior shrugged.

"But I suppose you'll have to satisfy yourselves. Are we under house arrest, or what?"

"Let's just say," said Chief of Police Dakin, "that we're all going to stay on for a few days till things kind of jell. I'll be in and out, but Mr. Queen and Herb Wentworth will be here to keep you company. The newspapers ain't onto this yet, so we ought to have ourselves a nice quiet time."

When the last upstairs light blinked out in the house, Ellery came up from the black lawn to the moon-whitened back porch and sat carefully down in a rocker.

Having known Bella Livingston in life, he wanted very much to pay his peculiar respects to her in death. She had deserved a better fate than smothering. But there was simply nothing to go on. He had told that to Chief Dakin before the chief left for the night. He had told Dakin something else, too, but the old Yank had been skeptical. "That ain't in the cards, Mr. Queen," Dakin had said, "not with you and Wentworth here." And he had added stubbornly, "Bella was an eighth-grader in the old Piney Road School when I was a skinny little firster, and she used to wipe my bloody nose when the big boys licked me. I ain't letting go of those three."

But it *was* in the cards.

What to do?

The sigh of the screen door and a gasp decided the question for him.

"It's only me, Miss Upham," Ellery said, getting up. "Too hot for sleep?"

"Hot?" Amy shivered as she sat down on the top step. "I couldn't imagine who was sitting out here." She drew her bathrobe more closely about her. "I'm glad it's you," she said suddenly.

"Oh? Why?"

"I don't know, I just am." She stared into the darkness. "Shouldn't I be?"

"Yes," Ellery said. "You should be very glad it's me."

She turned to him then. Something in the flat blacks and whites of his moonlit face made her swollen eyes widen.

Ellery sat down on the step beside her and took her little cold hands in his. "You strike me as a girl who's had to face up to a lot of disagreeable realities, Amy. I hope I'm not wrong. Because I'm going to throw the book at you."

"I don't understand."

"Bella Livingston made a tragic mistake when she wrote out that new will Friday night."

"Oh, I know! She should never have left me the money—"

"That wasn't her mistake. Her mistake, Amy, was in leaving you merely the income from it for your lifetime. And providing that thereafter the principal go to her stepchildren."

Amy looked bewildered. "She didn't want to cut them off altogether—"

"She also didn't know one of them would kill her in the belief that the old will was still in force." Ellery tightened his grip on her hands. "Amy," he said urgently, "lock your door at night. Try never to be alone." Her whole slender body strained about as she stared up at him. "That clause in the new will gives Bella Livingston's murderer a second chance. Because now the only thing that stands between him and a third of a million dollars is you."

Amy's face went white as the face of the moon. "He'd kill *me?*"

"Dakin and Wentworth don't think he'll risk it. I do. That's why I had to warn you."

She looked utterly lost. It made him touch her reassuringly, and his touch undid her.

He gathered her up in his arms, and she hung on to him, sobbing. "I'm afraid. I'm afraid . . ."

II

Even At The door of her room Amy would not let go of him.

"I know I'm being stupidly silly, but I can't help it . . ." Her teeth were chattering.

"How could you, after I've scared you half to death?" Ellery squeezed her arm. "Let's have a look together."

He searched her bedroom and bathroom. "Nobody here but us chickens," he said, and she smiled very faintly. "Now you lock and bolt your door and go to bed. I can get to you in five seconds from across the hall. All right, Amy?"

"All right," said Amy, and not altogether to his surprise she stood on tiptoe and kissed him. She flushed scarlet and pushed him into the hall.

He did not move from before her door until he heard the key turn over and the bolt slide into place.

Ellery made a groping tour of the sleeping rooms, soundlessly trying doors. Old Dorcas's and Morris Hunker's on the attic floor were unlocked, as was the door to the guest room where Mr. Wentworth snored melodiously. But the Livingston brothers had locked themselves in. He could hear them tossing about in their beds.

The door of their sister's room gave to his touch. He nudged it open, listening.

"Who is that?" Olivia's voice came out of the dark sharply.

"Oh," said Ellery. "Sorry. I thought this was my room."

He let the door click shut loudly.

She must sleep like a cat . . . It seemed to him, as he crawled into bed, that there was a mocking quality to the darkness.

He floundered and wallowed after sleep, his cheeks

still tingling where Amy had put her kiss. Lonely little thing . . . remarkably strong, too; his biceps ached where she had clutched him in her terror. Old Bella's money would make a full life possible for her . . . And sudden death, too, unless by some miracle he could perceive guilt where no guilt showed.

He kept straining after every sound in the old house until, exhausted, he fell asleep.

When he came downstairs Wednesday morning, Ellery found Olivia and Herbert Wentworth at breakfast.

"Ah, the man who mislaid his bedroom," said Olivia. "Did you ever find it, Mr. Detective?"

Ellery smiled back. "Your brothers still asleep?"

"Sam and Ev? They rarely roll out before noon."

"I wish Amy would get up," the lawyer said crossly. "I told her last night she'd have to sign some papers this morning. I've got to run over to the Court House."

"Just coffee, please, Dorcas." Ellery frowned. "Amy hasn't been down yet?"

"Oh, let the child sleep," said Olivia. "She'll collect her million a day later."

Mr. Wentworth glanced at her with dislike. "Dorcas—"

"Never mind Dorcas." Ellery jumped up. "I'll fetch her."

He had to force himself to walk sedately up the stairs. I've really got to stop acting like an old biddy, he thought, and knocked on Amy's door.

"Amy?"

He knocked again, harder.

"Amy." He tried the door; it was locked. "Amy?" He rattled the knob.

Doors opened. Everett Livingston's voice grumbled somewhere.

"Something wrong, Queen?" That was Samuel Junior.

"I don't know. Amy!" Ellery was pounding now.

Olivia and the Wrightsville lawyer came hurrying up the stairs. "What's the matter?"

"Help me with this damn door . . ."

At the second lunge the lock and bolt gave, and the door crashed back. Amy was lying on her bed in a queer position, very still.

"My God," said Wentworth.

"Is she . . . dead?" asked Olivia.

"No." Ellery was working over the unconscious girl. "Mr. Wentworth, phone a doctor—Conk Farnham, if you can get him. And Dakin. And have Dorcas come up immediately—I'll need her till the doctor comes. The rest of you—out!"

Dr. Conklin Farnham opened Amy's door. "It's all right to talk to her now."

They went into the bedroom. The late afternoon sun illuminated a bloodless Amy, propped on pillows and looking very young and small and lost in the big bed. A strapping woman with a football player's jaw, dressed in a nurse's uniform, sat by the bed.

Ellery took Amy's hand. It clutched.

"Feeling better now?"

"Lots." She tried to smile.

"What happened last night?"

"I don't know."

"I take it you didn't unlock your door or let anyone in. I found it locked this morning."

"I never went near it. I took a sleeping pill with some prune juice I had on my night table and went to bed. That's all I remember."

"The laboratory report indicates that you swallowed about six tablets. Luckily for you, not a lethal dose. You're positive you took only one before you went to bed?"

"Yes. I'm always careful about drugs—my Uncle Horace was a doctor and he taught me that. It came from a bottle in my medicine chest."

"We know, Amy," Chief Dakin said gently. "Who brought you the prune juice?"

"Nobody, Mr. Dakin. I'd poured it myself in the kitchen and taken it upstairs with me when I first started to go to bed. But I felt restless, so I went back downstairs, where I found Mr. Queen on the porch—"

"Leaving the glass of juice on the night table." Ellery glanced at Dakin. "I noticed it there when I brought Amy back up last night."

"By then it was doped." The old chief glowered. "Somebody snuck into her room while she was down on the back porch talking to you, and he fixed that prune juice just dandy . . . without leaving a print on anything."

"Mr. Queen," Amy said, "I'd like to talk to you."

"You'll do the rest of your talking tomorrow, young lady," said Dr. Farnham. "Now don't worry about her," he told them in the hall. "She'll be as good as new by morning. Mrs. Olin will stay with her all night."

On the way downstairs Chief Dakin said, "I guess I owe you an apology, Mr. Queen. I just never figured anyone'd try it."

"And I never thought to check that prune juice." Ellery scowled. "Dakin, is the nurse reliable?"

"Libby Olin?" Dakin snorted. "It's a brave man who'd try to get past *her*."

They found the Livingston trio sprawled in the drawing room, waiting peacefully under the codfish eye of Mr. Wentworth and one of Chief Dakin's brawnier young policemen.

"She's going to be all right, Mr. Wentworth," Ellery said; and he turned to the Livingstons with his bitterness showing. "Whichever one of you tried to overdose Amy last night took a losing gamble. She's very much alive, and there are a number of us in this house who are dedicated to the proposition that she's going to stay that way."

"From now on," growled the chief of police, "Amy Upham's going to be guarded twenty-four hours a day."

"A smart poker player knows when his luck's run out," Ellery told the silent three. "You can't win that million any more, but you can stand pat on the gamble that we won't be able to call you for Bella Livingston's murder or the attempt on Amy."

"And don't be thinking that because we haven't called you yet," added Dakin, "you can pick up and run." His Yankee jaw aimed at them. "You ain't setting a pinkie toe off these grounds. Not one of you."

"You know," murmured Samuel Livingston, Junior, "you fellows amaze me. How long do you suppose you could hold us here if we insisted on leaving? You have absolutely no grounds for this."

"And for the simplest of reasons," Olivia said and smiled. "We haven't done anything."

"What's keeping us here," chimed in Everett, "is a temporary embarrassment and the three crude but nourishing meals a day."

"In my case it's rather more than that." The elder brother set his drink down with a little bang and looked up at Ellery and Chief Dakin with no charm whatever. "In the beginning your accusations were on the amusing side, but the humor has begun to pall. I'm feeling persecuted, gentlemen, and it's a feeling I don't care for."

"On top of which," said Olivia, "a Livingston never tucks his tail between his legs."

"Besides," said Everett with a grin, "you might just clap us in the pokey. In the present state of my finances, a suit for false arrest would buy me that basketball franchise."

"Neat," said Ellery. "Even convincing. But I repeat —don't crowd your luck."

He strode out with a self-confident righteousness he did not feel.

"I can't say I blame you, Amy," Ellery said.

"Well, I've had lots of time to think since yesterday." Amy looked out over the lawn. Ellery kicked one of the loose floorboards.

It was Thursday afternoon, and they were sitting in the old summerhouse on the back lawn. The young policeman was fidgeting under a tree nearby. The sun through the latticework checkered Amy's hollow cheeks and frightened eyes in a grotesque pattern. She kept staring out through the summerhouse doorway. The rear windows of the big mansion shimmered like eyes.

"We could let them go, of course," Ellery grumbled.

"And suppose one of them sneaked back next week? Or next year, for that matter!" Amy shook her head. "Don't you see, Mr. Queen, I'd never have another day's peace for the rest of my life?"

"I can only tell you that we're checking them exhaustively. If we find that one of them is not merely broke but desperately in debt, it will pinpoint a murder motive. And I've had Dakin send the file of prints up to Boston as a check on the Connhaven laboratory." Ellery scowled at the dappled floor. "I don't want to influence you, Amy. It's your life. But a step like this would be irrevocable."

"You think I'm a coward."

"No."

"It's not the thought of dying. I'm sort of used to death. My father and mother, Uncle Horace, now Mother Livingston . . ." Amy bit her lip. "It's the *waiting* for it. Never knowing when the ax will fall. And I mean ax."

Amy rose and went to the doorway. In her white summer frock the sunlight gave her a fragile transparency uncomfortably ghostlike. "I couldn't live a life like that, Mr. Queen. I'm going back to the house and tell them they can have it all."

Ellery sprang.

The flash from the attic window and his leap were almost simultaneously. But the rifle crack reached his ears even as he bowled Amy over onto the grass and covered her with his body.

The policeman was running toward the house, tugging at his holster.

Ellery twisted his neck for a look. The attic window from which the flash had come was empty.

"What happened?" Amy's voice came muffled, but calmly.

"You're not hit?" he demanded.

"Only by you."

He helped her to her feet and glanced about, baffled. Then he saw it.

The bullet had ripped through the summerhouse roof a good eight feet above and beyond where Amy's head had been.

Ellery came downstairs with the rifle just as the policeman was hanging up the phone in the entrance hall.

"Chief's coming right away, Mr. Queen."

"Have you talked to Dorcas and Morris?"

"They didn't see a thing. They were both in the kitchen, Dorcas fixing a chicken pie for supper and Morris washing the lunch dishes. All they did was duck."

Ellery found Mr. Wentworth in the drawing room, pounding fist on palm, his incensed length between Amy and the Livingstons as if to shield her from a head-on attack.

"I'm good and darn tired of this pocus!" the lawyer was shouting. "You let this girl be, ye hear?"

"Mr. Wentworth, you bore the hell out of me." Olivia's cheeks were splotchy with anger. She was in shorts and a halter, and her skin looked oiled.

Her brothers were glaring.

Ellery stepped into the room. The policeman blocked the doorway.

"Sam Livingston's gun," Ellery said, holding it up. "It has his name plate on the butt."

"Father's old deer rifle!" Samuel Junior half rose.

"Mother Livingston wouldn't part with it." Amy sounded so grimly self-assured that Ellery glanced at her. "She kept it in the attic storeroom."

"Where I found it, dropped near the window. Plus an old box of ammo freshly broken into. When the chief gets here we'll have the gun and box gone over." Ellery set the rifle down with care. "While we're waiting for him, suppose I put the classic question: Where were you three when the shot was fired?"

Olivia shrilled, "I was on the roof taking a sunbath."

"Alone?"

"Since I sunbathe in the nude, Mr. Queen, it's hardly likely that I held a soiree!"

"Fair enough." Ellery glanced at Everett, who was no longer looking at Amy with anticipation. Everett no longer looked at Amy at all.

"I'd been down to the pond for a swim," the chunky brother grunted, "and I was back in the house under a shower at the time the shot is supposed to have been fired. You couldn't prove it by me. I heard nothing but running water." His thick body was wrapped in a damp terry-cloth robe.

"And I was seated right here, Mr. Queen, listening to a newscast." Samuel Junior's nostrils were on the pinched side. "By the way, I haven't fired a gun in fifteen years —it's a sport for brutes. And I'm sure my sister and brother couldn't hit their own reflections in a mirror."

"Neither could the one who shot at Amy," Ellery remarked. "Mr. Wentworth, did you happen to see any of these people?"

"Not soon enough to give any of 'em an alibi," snapped the Yankee lawyer. "The shot woke me from a nap, and by the time I got my shoes on they were congregated in the upstairs hall. Mr. Queen, if Dakin keeps these people on the premises after *this*—!"

"Before we go into the matter of improved security, I believe Amy has an announcement. Amy?"

"No."

"*No?*"

"I've changed my mind." Amy was returning the Livingstons' stares with compound interest. "I *was* going to sign everything over to you three after one of you tried to kill me with those sleeping pills. But now I'm *mad*. If you want that money, you're going to have to shoot a lot straighter that you shot today. Because I'm not going to be scared off."

Ellery was gaping at her. "What did you say, Amy?"

"I said, Mr. Queen, they're not going to scare me any more."

Olivia rose. "Really, I've had just about as much of this—!"

"Please sit down." Ellery was still staring at Amy Upham. Then he said slowly, "Officer, nobody is to leave this room until Chief Dakin gets here."

He stumbled past the policeman and disappeared.

"There you are." Dakin shut the door of Bella Livingston's bedroom. "No prints on the gun or box of shells, no clues in the attic, no *anything*," he said in disgust. But then he stopped, struck by Ellery's silence.

Ellery was crouched at the old lady's Governor Winthrop desk in the bay overlooking the front lawn. The room had been sealed up since the murder, and his hands were dusty. He had pulled open all the drawers and dumped their contents on the desk—letters, household bills, canceled checks, various kinds of stationery, old invitations to Wrightsville functions—the accumulation of years. But he was not looking at them; his glance was fixed on something not visible to Chief Dakin.

"Something *else* wrong, Mr. Queen?"

"What?" Ellery turned slowly around. "Oh, Dakin. Sit down. I want to talk to you."

Mr. Wentworth was just taking the candlewick spread off his bed Friday night when someone tapped furtively on his door.

"Yes? Who is it?"

"Amy." Her whisper was urgent. "Quick."

The lawyer yanked his door open, alarmed. "What's the trouble?"

"Shh! I can't stay but a second—"

"Are you out of your mind, Amy? After we locked you in for the night!"

"Please, I've got to talk to you, Mr. Wentworth. Just *you.*"

"Me? Now?"

"Not now— that policeman keeps trying my door every few minutes. Meet me at the pond tomorrow morning early—say six o'clock. Will you? Please?" Amy's brown eyes kept searching the hall. "You've got to, Mr. Wentworth," she whispered fiercely. "*Will* you?"

The lawyer was bewildered. "But Amy—"

But Amy was gone.

Mr. Wentworth hurried through Bella Livingston's woods in the damp of early morning Saturday, shivering. He had tossed about all night, perplexed and uneasy. What could Amy Upham possibly have to confide in him that Queen and the chief of police mustn't hear?

And why, he suddenly thought, in such an out-of-the-way spot?

The lawyer found himself wanting very much to turn back. *It's almost as though I were in danger* . . .

But that was ridiculous.

Mr. Wentworth shivered again and broke into a trot. He heard Amy's scream just as the pond began to glitter through the birch and scrub oak and pine.

"Help! Somebody! Help!"

The lawyer scrambled out on the tumble-down landing. The Livingston rowboat lay fifty yards offshore, deep in the water and settling fast. Amy was trying frantically to row through a patch of water lilies.

"Mr. Wentworth!" she shrieked. "*Somebody put a hole in the boat and I can't swim!*"

All of a sudden the boat sank and Amy sank with it.

Mr. Wentworth gasped. He kicked off his shoes in a panicky haste and dived in. When he surfaced, he saw Amy thrashing about and making glubbing sounds.

"Hang on to the boat! I'll be right there!" he yelled. He made directly for her, swimming as fast as he could against the drag of his clothing. She went under again just as he reached her. She came up spluttering, clutching at him, tangled up in the lilies. "Let *go*, Amy!" Mr. Wentworth panted. "I've got you—you won't drown . . ." He had to fight her all the way back to the landing. By the time he had her safely out of the pond he was exhausted.

"You—all—right?" he panted.

"You all right, Amy?" a male voice echoed.

"Yes," said Amy; and Mr. Wentworth squirmed about in his wet things, mouth open. Two men stood almost directly behind him. His heart jumped; but then he saw who they were.

"Queen, Dakin." He staggered to his feet gladly. "Hole in the boat—they tried to drown her—I had to jump in after her—"

"We know," said Ellery. "We saw the whole thing."

"You . . . *saw*—?"

"In fact," Chief Dakin said, "you might say it was kind of a trap."

"Trap." The lawyer shook his head in a dazed way. "I don't understand. Trap?"

Ellery squatted on a log and lit a cigaret. "You're certainly entitled to an explanation, Mr. Wentworth. Right, Amy?"

But Amy said nothing. She was sitting Indian-fashion on the landing, shaking out her blond hair.

"Thursday afternoon, Mr. Wentworth," Ellery said, "Amy remarked in the drawing room that she wasn't going to be 'scared' out of her inheritance. I blush to confess that that hadn't occurred to me—that the non-lethal dose of sleeping pills and the rifle shot that missed so wildly were actually attempts, not to kill Amy, but to *frighten* her—scare her into giving up the estate. It was the wrong hypothesis, as it turned out, but without it I probably wouldn't have arrived at the right one."

"Maybe you know what you're talking about," said the Wrightsville lawyer testily, "but I surely don't."

"We'd been taking it for granted that Bella Livingston's killer was also out to kill Amy," Ellery went on, surveying Amy's graceful gestures. "But suppose he

hasn't been? Suppose he's only been trying to make it
look that way? That's what I asked myself. And I saw
that so long as we kept assuming that Amy also was
meant to be murdered, the motive continued to point to
the three Livingstons, the only people who'd benefit
from Amy's death. But . . . if Amy was *not* really
meant to be murdered, then the whole assumption of the
Livingstons' guilt was out of joint and we had to re-ex-
amine the case from the beginning.

"Which is precisely what I did, Mr. Wentworth. I
went back to Bella Livingston's will."

Amy was stripping off her dress quite calmly. There
was a bathing suit under it, and much sun-burnished
skin. Mr. Wentworth gaped.

"It struck me at once what a curious-*looking* will that
is," Ellery said dreamily. "With all sorts of writing paper
to choose from—I checked old Bella's desk in her bedroom—her will was nevertheless written on onionskin
paper. Why *onionskin*, a paper so thin it's translucent?
Translucent . . . you can see through it, especially in
the light—use it as tracing paper. Tracing paper! Was it
possible the old lady had written her new will on ordi-
nary paper, *but someone had traced over it and substi-
tuted the tracing for the original?*"

Ellery flicked his cigaret into the pond. "You see how
one thought led to another, Mr. Wentworth. Now—assuming I was right, why a *tracing* of old Bella's will?
Obviously, to make a change. A simple change, of
course; because a complex one—as in forming new
words—would have required the tracer to be an expert
forger, in this case a most remote possibility.

"What simple change? I recalled that the will gave, as
the approximate value of Mrs. Livingston's principal estate, the figure $1,000,000. Then it came to me: Sup-
pose the will had given the value of the estate, not as
$1,000,000, but as $4,000,000, or $7,000,000, or even
$9,000,000? How easy it would be, in a tracing, to leave
out the wedge of the 4, or the horizontal stroke of the 7,
or the loop of the 9. Then 4, 7, or 9 becomes 1, and a

multimillion-dollar estate becomes a million-dollar estate.

"And that led to a remarkable conclusion, Mr. Wentworth. For who could have made such a tracing? Why, only the person who had possession of the new will from Saturday morning, when Bella Livingston signed it before witnesses in his office, until Tuesday afternoon, when he produced the tracing after the funeral and purported it to be the original. Also, who would benefit by such a change? Strangely enough, one person and only one—the same man who had exclusive possession of the new will—the man who's been handling Bella Livingston's financial affairs for years and who's named administrator of her estate."

Herbert Wentworth squatted like a terrified toad on the landing.

"You're not half your father's son, Wentworth," said Ellery. "Your father, from what I've heard of him, would have cut his right hand off before he touched a penny of any moneys entrusted to him.

"But you couldn't resist the opportunity handed to you on a golden platter. You had the new will, its contents unknown. You had the stock and the bonds and the records. And in old Bella's house were three live suspects, if anything should happen to her. So you stole into her house at three A.M. last Sunday, crept into her bedroom, and smothered her in her sleep—knowing that you had until Tuesday to make a tracing of her holograph will and change the figure she had written down to a 1 . . . giving you the balance to pocket and all the time in the world—you thought—to cover your tracks."

"Only you didn't make it, Herb," said Chief Dakin in his sternly sorrowful way. "I've had lawyers from the State's Attorney's office working on this behind your back since Thursday night. They've already turned up enough to show that the estate's worth four million easy. And of course we just took that onionskin will back from the Court of Probate and handed it over to experts. Why, Herb, you left a fingerprint *under* some of the tracing." The old chief shook his head. "And when we opened your safe deposit box by court order yesterday, we even found the original of Bella's new will. Now why in the world did you save that, Herb? I guess it ain't so easy to change the honest habits of a lifetime even when you turn crook."

The droplets dripping from the lawyer's clothes began to scatter in their fall.

Amy turned away to look at the pond.

"Finally," Ellery said, "those two attempts on Amy's life. I knew you'd killed Bella, Wentworth; but I was only assuming you'd dosed Amy's prune juice and fired the shot at her from the attic window in order to cast further suspicion on the Livingstons. If my assumption was correct, your attempts on Amy were deliberate phonies. If my assumption was correct, you didn't want her to die—in fact, you'd go a long way to preserve her life, because if Amy were murdered within days of Bella's murder it would be bound to bring that traced will back under close scrutiny.

"So," said Ellery, "I got Amy to stage that little drowning scene this morning to see what you would do. And you did it, Wentworth—you nearly drowned yourself in your anxiety to keep her alive. By the way, Amy can swim like a dolphin."

"And I think that's about it, Herb," said Chief Dakin after a while, "except," he added, "for the disagreeable part."

They sat in a communion of silence while Herbert Wentworth stumbled off through the woods followed by the comments of the birds and the sad clump of Dakin's shoes.

"Poor Mr. Wentworth," Amy said at last.

"Poor Mr. Queen," mumbled Ellery. "What in heaven's name am I going to say to those three back at the house, Amy? They've taken a pretty rough beating."

"Oh, I don't think they'll mind," Amy said. "I mean, after *I've* talked to them. You see, I've been thinking . . ."

"Not again," Ellery said in some dismay.

"No, really. How could I possibly spend more than one-fourth of the income from four million dollars?" Amy put her palms down on the landing behind her and threw her blond head back to the sun. "Isn't it a lovely day?"

Ellery looked down into her brown, brown eyes.

"Lovely," he said.

DIAMONDS
in
PARADISE

MAYBE LILI MINX used to be the girl of your dreams, too. It's nothing to be ashamed of. Lili caused more insomnia in her day than all the midnight maatjes herring consumed on Broadway and 51st Street on all the opening nights put together since Jenny Lind raised the gulls off the roof of Castle Garden.

It wasn't just Lili's face and figure, either, although she could have drifted out on a bare apron before a two-bit vaudeville flat and stood there for two hours and twenty minutes merely looking at you, and you'd have headed for your herring, shouting, "Smash hit!" It wasn't even her voice, which made every other set of female pipes on Broadway sound like something ground out of a box with a monkey on it. It was the way she had of making every male within eyeshot feel that he was alone with her in a dreamboat.

Of course, it was a trick, and you can't run up an inside report on the magician by a study of his act; ask the seven dreamboat captains she divorced.

The truth was, La Minx was a mixed-up kid with a lot of wonderful equipment that, practically speaking, didn't mean a thing. She put in a great deal of paid-up couch time trying to find out what made her run, but who cared? It was enough for every man but her ex-husbands and her analyst to watch her walk onstage—and, at that, her analyst was by no means a sure thing.

One of Lili's problems was diamonds. She was hipped on diamonds.

It wasn't avarice. Lili could drop fifty grand at the roulette wheel and stroll away yawning. But the mislaying of a single chip from her hoard of diamonds sent her into hysterics; even off the record her press agent swore that she checked her inventory every night before going to bed.

In the beginning Lili Minx's collection was the natural target of every creep out of the jug. But after a few of them tangled with her, Lili was declared out of bounds. She once spent $23,000 in private-detective fees tracking down a panicky jewel thief who had been unlucky enough to succeed in lifting a diamond ring of hers worth fifteen hundred; she caught him, got her ring back, and then vamped the judge into hurling the book at him. The light-fingered lads passed the word that it was a surer thing putting the snatch on the gold in the President's teeth than trying to get away with the lousiest bauble in Lili's jewel box. When it came to her diamonds, Lil could have told Javert things about the sewers of Paris he never knew.

But there are always operators who can't resist the glitter made by a buzz-saw; and this is the story of one such.

It happened in Paradise Gardens, Lili's favorite gambling hell. Paradise Gardens enjoyed a brief glory in the days when New York was wide open, club doors had peepholes for dramatic effect, and everything went, usually with great speed. The Paradise masqueraded behind a frowzy old brownstone front in the East Fifties off Fifth Avenue.

Inside, the azure ceiling twinkled with stars and well-developed angels, you sat among tripical flowers under papier-mâché trees with apples tied to their branches, and your food and potables were served by show-girl type waitresses wearing imitation fig leaves. But if you were known to be able to write expensive checks with no bounce, you could go upstairs. Upstairs there was no mullarkey about Gardens or Edens, just nice business décor to set off the green baize-covered tables at which the management permitted you to lose large sums of money.

Lili Minx was between husbands, and on this particular evening she was alone. She floated in, pale-perfect in white velvet and ermine—remote as the Pleiades and appetizing as a charlotte russe. On each little ear burned a cold green fire, La Minx's only jewelry tonight. They were the famous Mumtaz green diamond earrings, once the property of Shah Jahan's favorite sultana, which had been clipped to Lili's lobes by the quivering hands of an Iraqi millionaire under the delusion that he was about to enjoy an Arabian Nights entertainment. Lili prized them at least as highly as the ears to which they were attached.

Everything stopped as Lili paused in the archway for her moment of tribute; then play was resumed, and Lili bought a stack of thousand-dollar chips at the cashier's cage and went to the roulette table.

An hour later her second stack was in the croupier's bank. Lili laughed and drifted off toward the ladies' lounge, her slender fingers to her forehead delicately. No one spoke to her.

The chic French maid in the lounge came forward swiftly. "Madame has the headache?"

"Yes."

"Perhaps some aspirin and a cold compress?"

"Please."

Lili lay down on a chaise longue and closed her eyes. It was bad tonight, very bad. The cold touch of the wrapped icebag on her forehead felt delicious; she smiled her thanks. The maid, deftly and in sympathetic silence, adjusted the pillow under her head. It was quiet in the lounge, and Lili slipped off into her own world of dreams.

She awoke a few minutes later, her headache almost gone. Lili put the icebag aside and rose from the chaise. The maid had discreetly vanished.

La Minx went to a vanity and sat down to fix her hair . . .

At that exact moment the gambling rooms of Paradise Gardens went berserk. Women shrieked, their escorts skittered about like trapped mice, the housemen struggled with their wheels and faro and crap layouts, and the massive door gave way under the axheads of police.

"Hold it, everybody!" A small elderly man with a gray mustache hopped nimbly onto a crap table and held up his arms for silence. "I'm Inspector Queen of police headquarters on special gambling detail. Ladies and gentlemen, this is a raid. Don't waste your time trying to get away; every exit is covered. Now if you'll all please line up along the walls while the officers go to work—"

And that was when Lili Minx burst from the ladies' lounge, looking like one of the Furies and screaming, "My diamond earrings! *I've been robbed!*"

No one was surprised that what had begun as a gambling raid should turn immediately into a robbery investigation—no one, that is, who knew the Minx. She swept everything before her like a natural force. Dazzled by the lightning in those heavenly eyes, bowing to the hurricane in that golden-trumpeting voice, Inspector Queen did her bidding as eagerly as Moses on the Mount. She had often enough disturbed his dreams, too.

As the axes rose and fell and the equipment splintered, the Inspector crooned, "Now don't you worry your pretty little head, Miss Minx, we'll find your earrings—"

"You're moddang right you will!" stormed Lili. "And that moddang maid, too! She's the only one touched me! I want her *scrotched!*"

"She can't get away, Miss Minx," the old fire-eater beamed, patting the lovely little hand. "We've had the Paradise surrounded for an hour getting set for this jump, and not one soul's left the premises. So she has to be here. Well, Velie?" he barked as the big sergeant came loping out of the ladies' lounge feeling his tie furtively. "Where is that moddang maid?"

"Right here, Inspector." Sergeant Velie, looking at Lili like a lovelorn Newfoundland, dumped into the Inspector's arms a maid's uniform, a starched cap and apron, a pair of high-heeled shoes, two sheer stockings, and a brunette wig. "I found them in the lounge broom closet."

Lili glared at the wig. "What does this mean?"

"Why, it's Harry the Actor," said the Inspector, pleased. "A clever little skunk at female impersonation, Miss Minx—he's made his finest hauls as a French maid. So Harry's pulled it on you, has he? You just wait here, my dear." And the old gent began to march along the line-up at the wall like a wiry little Fate, followed by La Minx, who took orders from no one where her jewels were concerned.

"And here he is," said the Inspector cheerily, stopping before a slender man with the build of a jockey and boyish cheeks that were very pale at the moment. "Tough luck, Harry—the raid, I mean. Suppose we try this on for size, shall we?" and Inspector Queen clapped the brunette wig on the small man's head.

"That'sssss . . . the one," hissed Lili Minx; and the little thief turned a shade paler, which the Inspector would have said was impossible. The actress stepped up to Harry so that they stood chest to chest, and she looked deep into his eyes.

"You give me back my diamond earrings, you exanzebious thus-and-so, or I'll tear off your . . ." Lili went into considerable detail, chiefly anatomical.

"Get her away from me," quavered Harry the Actor in his girlish treble, trying to burrow into the wall.

"Search him, Velie," said Inspector Queen hastily.

In the manager's office a half hour later, with the window drapes drawn, Harry the Actor stood shivering in a September Morn attitude, peeled to the buff. On the manager's desk lay everything taken from his person: a wallet containing several hundred dollars, a pocketful of change, a ball-point pen, a racing form, a pair of battered old dice, a pack of cigarets and a booklet of matches, a vial of French perfume, a lipstick, a compact, a handkerchief smeared with make-up, and a box of Kis-Mee, the Magic Breath Sweetner. Everything in parts had been disassembled. The cigarets had been shredded. The little thief's clothing had been gone over seam by seam. His shoes had been tapped for hidden compartments. His mouth and hair had been carefully probed. Various indignities had been visited upon his person, and not only upon it. Even the abandoned maid's outfit had been examined.

The green diamond earrings were not found.

The Inspector growled, "All right, Houdini. Get dressed."

And all the while, from the other side of the manager's door, La Minx's delicious voice could be heard, promising Harry the Actor what was in store for him when *she* got her hands on him.

It drove the poor man at last to a desperate performance. In the act of restoring his belongings to his pockets, he suddenly vaulted over the desk, stiff-armed the policeman before the window, and leaped through the drapes like a mountain goat. It was an unlucky night for Harry all around. The railing of the fire escape was rotten with rust. His momentum took him into space, carrying the railing with him. They heard the railing land on the concrete of the back yard three stories below, then the soggy thud that was Harry.

The officers posted in the yard were shaking their heads over the little thief when Inspector Queen and Sergeant Velie dropped off the fire escape, followed—incredibly—by Lili Minx.

If Harry the Actor had had any hope of cheating his karma, one glazed look at the furious beauty glaring down at him destroyed it. Either way he was a goner, and he knew it.

"Harry," said Inspector Queen, tapping the livid cheek gently, "you're checking out, and you'd better speak up if you want a fair shake Upstairs. Where did you stash 'em?"

Harry's eyes rolled; his tongue appeared. It quivered a little. Then he said thickly, "Diamonds . . . in . . . Paradise . . ."

"In the Paradise *what,* Harry? *Where?*"

But Harry had had it.

Ellery always said that if it wasn't his greatest case, it certainly was his shortest.

He first learned about it when the Inspector staggered home at breakfast time. Ellery got some coffee into him and extracted the baffling details.

"And I tell you, son," croaked his father, "we went back into that joint and tore it apart. It was rotten luck, Harry's dying before he could tell us exactly where in the Paradise Gardens he'd hidden Lili's diamonds. They had to be in the building somewhere, either in something or on someone. We still hadn't let anyone go from the raid; and we not only took the Paradise apart bit by bit, we body-searched every mother's son and daughter on the premises, thinking Harry might have passed the earrings on to an accomplice. Well, we didn't find them." Inspector Queen sounded as if he were going to cry. "I don't know what I'll say to that sweet child."

Ellery reflected. Finally he said in a businesslike way, "Dad, I'll make a deal with you."

"Deal?" his father said, bewildered. "What deal?"

"If I tell you where Harry the Actor hid those earrings, may I deliver them to the sweet child personally?"

"Well . . ." said the senior Queen. But then he howled, "But how can you know? You weren't even there!"

"Harry was stowing the contents of his pockets away, you said, when he took that Nijinsky jump. Where is he now, Dad?"

"Where would he be in his condition?" the old man grumbled. "In the Morgue!"

"Then the Morgue is where you'll find Lili's earrings."

"You mean they *were* on him? But, Ellery, we searched Harry outside and—and in!"

"Tell me again what he had in his pockets."

"Money, a dirty handkerchief, cosmetics, a racing form, a pair of dice, cigarets, matches—"

"I quote you quoting the late Actor's dying statement," said Ellery. And he said deliberately, " 'Diamonds . . . in . . . Paradise.' "

"Diamonds in Paradise," the Inspector repeated, wiggling his brows. "So?"

"Paradise," said Ellery. "Pair o' dice."

"Pair o' dice . . . Pair of *dice?*"

"Trick dice," Ellery nodded. "Hollowed out. Diamonds inside. Give me a note to the Morgue property clerk, Dad," Ellery said briskly, looking himself over in the mirror. "I mustn't keep the lady waiting."

"Pair of dice," his father said feebly. "But it sounded just like the word Paradise . . ."

"What do you expect from a dying man," said Ellery, handing the Inspector paper and pen, "elocution lessons?"

The
CASE AGAINST
CARROLL

CARROLL FELT THE heat through his shoes as he got out of the taxi. In the swollen twilight even the Park across Fifth Avenue had a look of suffering. It made him worry again about how Helena was taking the humidity.

"What?" Carroll said, reaching for his wallet. It was a thirty-six-birthday present from Helena, and he usually challenged taxi drivers to identify the leather, which was elephant hide. But tonight's hack was glowering at the slender gray-stone building with its fine-boned black balconies.

"I said," the driver said, "that's your house?"

"Yes." Carroll immediately felt angry. The lie of convenience had its uses, but on days like this it stung. The gray-stone had been erected in the Seventies by Helena's great-grandfather, and it belonged to her.

"Air-conditioned, no doubt," the man said, wiping out his ear. "How would you like to live in one of them de luxe East Side hotboxes on a night like this?"

"No, thank you," Carroll said, remembering.

"I got four kids down there, not to mention my old lady. What do you think of that?"

Carroll overtipped him.

He used his key on the bronze street door with a sense of sanctuary. The day had been bad all around, expecially at Hunt, West & Carroll, Attorneys-at-Law. Miss Mallowan, his secretary, had chosen this day to throw her monthly fainting spell; the new clerk had wasted three hours conscientiously looking up the wrong citations; Meredith Hunt, playing the senior partner with a heavy hand, had been at his foulest; and Tully West, ordinarily the most urbane of men, had been positively short-tempered at finding himself with only one change of shirt in the office. Trickling through the day, acidlike, had been Carroll's worry about Helena. He had telephoned twice, and she had been extra-cheery both times. When Helena sounded extra-cheery, she was covering up something.

Had she found out?

But that wasn't possible.

Unless Tully . . .

But Carroll shook his head, wincing. Tully West couldn't know. Tully's code coupled snooping with using the wrong fork and other major crimes.

It's the weather, Carroll decided fatuously; and he stepped into his wife's house.

Indoors, he felt a little better. The house with its crystal chandeliers, Italian marble, and shimmering floors was as cameo-cool as Helena herself—as all the Vanowens must have been, judging from the Sargents lording it over the walls. He had never stopped feeling grateful that they were all defunct except Helena. The Vanowens went back to the patroons, while he was the son of a trackwalker from the New York transit system who had been killed by a subway train while tilting a bottle on the job. Breeding had been the Vanowens' catchword; they would not have cared for Helena's choice of husband.

John Carroll deposited his hat and briefcase in the

foyer closet and trudged upstairs, letting his wet palm squeak along the satiny rail.

Helena was in the upstairs sitting room, reading *Winnie the Pooh* for the umpteenth time to Breckie and Louanne.

And she was in the wheelchair again.

Carroll watched his wife's face from the archway as she made the absurd Eeyore sounds the children never tired of. Through the angry stab of helplessness he felt the old wonder. Her slender body was bunched, tight in defense, against the agony of her arthritis-racked legs, but that delicate face under its coif of auburn was as serene as a nun's. Only he knew what a price she paid for that serenity.

"Daddy, it's Daddy!"

Two rockets flew at him. Laden down with sleepered arms and legs, Carroll went to his wife and kissed her.

"Now, darling," Helena said.

"How bad is it?" he growled.

"Not bad. John, you're soaked. Did you have to work so late in this swelter?"

"I suppose that's why you're in the wheelchair."

"I've had Mrs. Poole keep dinner hot for you."

"Mommy let us stay up because we were so *good*," Louanne said. "Now can we have the choc-o-late, Daddy?"

"We weren't so *very* good," Breckie said. "See, see, Louanne, I told you Daddy wouldn't forget!"

"We'll help you take your shower." Helena strained forward in the wheelchair. "Breckie angel, your bottom's sticking out. John, really. Couldn't you have made it Lifesavers today?"

"It's bad, isn't it?"

"A little," Helena admitted, smiling.

A little! thought Carroll as they all went upstairs in the lift he had had installed two years before, when Helena's condition had become chronic. A little—when even at the best of times she had to drag about like an old woman. And, on crutches or in the wheelchair, refusing to let others bring up her children . . .

He showered in full view of his admiring family, impotently aware of the health of his long, dark body.

When he pattered back to the bedroom he found a shaker of martinis and, on his bed, fresh linen and his favorite slacks and jacket.

"What's the matter, John?"

Carroll said tenderly, "I didn't think it showed."

He kissed her on the chocolate smudge left by Breckie's fingers.

Like a character in a bad TV drama, Hunt came with the thunder and the rain.

Carroll was surprised. He was also embarrassed by the abrupt way the children stopped chattering as the lawyer's thick-set figure appeared in the dining-room doorway.

"Meredith." Carroll half rose. "I thought you were on your way to Chicago."

"I'm headed for La Guardia now," Hunt said. "Legs again, Helena?"

"Yes. Isn't it a bore?" Helena glanced at the housekeeper, who was in the foyer holding Hunt's wet things at arm's length. "Mr. Hunt will take coffee with us, Mrs. Poole."

"Yes, ma'am."

"No, ma'am," Meredith Hunt said. "But I thank you. *And* the Carroll small-fry. Up kind of late, aren't you?"

Breckie and Louanne edged stealthily toward their mother's chair.

"We like to wait up for our daddy." Helena smiled, drawing them to her. "How's Felicia, Meredith? I must call her as soon as this lets up a bit."

"Don't. My wife is being very Latin-American these days."

Something was terribly wrong. Looking back on the day, John Caroll felt another thrill of alarm.

Helena said extra-cheerily, "Way past your bedtime,

bunny rabbits! Kiss you father and say good night to Mr. Hunt."

She herded them out with her wheelchair. As she turned the chair into the foyer, she glanced swiftly at her husband. Then she said something crisp to Mrs. Poole, and they all disappeared behind the clang of the lift door.

Carroll said, "Life's little surprises. You wanted to talk to me, Meredith?"

"Definitely." Hunt's large teeth glistened.

"Let's go up to my study."

"I can talk here."

Carroll looked at him. "What's on your mind?"

"You're a crook," Meredith Hunt said.

Carroll sat down. He reached with concentration for the crystal cigaret box on the table.

"When did you find out, Meredith?"

"I knew I was making a mistake the day I let Tully West pull that *noblesse oblige* act for Helena and sweet-talk me into taking you into the firm." The burly lawyer sauntered about the dining room, eyeing the marble fireplace, the painting, the crystal cabinets, the heirloom silver. "You can't make a blue ribbon entry out of an alley accident, I always say. The trouble with Tully and Helena, John, is that they're sentimental idiots. They really believe in democracy."

The flame of the lighter shivered. Carroll put the cigaret down unlit.

"I wish you'd let me explain, Meredith."

"So I've kept an eye on you," Hunt said, not pausing in his stroll. "And especially on the Eakins Trust. It's going to give me a lot of satisfaction to show my blue-blood partner just how and when his mongrel protégé misappropriated twenty thousand dollars' worth of trust securities."

"Will you let me explain?"

"Explain away. Horses? The market?" Hunt swung about. A nerve in the heavy flesh beneath his right eye was jumping. "A woman?"

"Keep your voice down, Meredith."

"A woman. Sure. When a man like you is married to a—"

"Don't!" Carroll said. Then he said, "Does Tully know?"

"Not yet."

"It was my brother Harry. He got into a dangerous mess involving some hard characters, and he had to get out in a hurry. He needed twenty thousand dollars to square himself, and he came to me for it."

"And you stole it for him."

"I told him I didn't have it. I don't have it. My take from the firm just about keeps our heads above water. It's my income runs this house, Meredith. Or did you think I let Helena's money feed me, too? Anyway, Harry threatened to go to Helena for it."

"And, of course," Hunt said, showing his teeth again, "you couldn't let him do that."

"No," Carroll said. "No, Meredith, I couldn't. I don't expect you to understand why. Helena wouldn't hesitate to give me any amount I asked for, but . . . Well, I had no way of borrowing a wad like that overnight except to go to you and/or Tully. Tully was somewhere in northern Canada hunting, and to go to you . . ." Carroll paused. When he looked up he said, "So I took it from the Eakins Trust, proving your point."

Meredith Hunt nodded with enjoyment.

Carroll pushed himself erect on his fists. "I've got to ask you to give me time. I'll replace the funds by the first of the year. It won't happen again, Meredith. Harry's in Mexico, and he won't be back. It won't happen again. The first of the year." He swallowed. "Please," he said.

"Monday," Hunt said.

"What?"

"This is Friday. I'll give you till Monday morning to make up the defalcation. You have sixty hours to keep from arrest, prison, and disbarment. If you replace the money I'll drop the matter to protect the firm. In any event, of course, you're through at the office."

"Monday." Carroll laughed. "Why not tonight? It would be just as merciful."

"You can get the money from your wife. Or from Tully, if he's stupid enough to give it to you."

"I won't drag Helena into this!" Carroll heard his voice rising, and he pulled it down with an effort. "Or Tully—I value his friendship too much. I got myself into this jam, and all I'm asking is the chance to get myself out."

"That's your problem. I'm being very generous, under the circumstances." All the lines of Hunt's well-preserved face sagged as his cold eyes flamed with sudden heat. "Especially since the Eakins Trust isn't the only property you haven't been able to keep your hands off."

"What's that supposed to mean?"

"Your sex life is your own business as long as you don't poach on mine. Stay away from my wife."

Carroll's fist caught Hunt on the right side of the mouth. Blood trickled down Hunt's big chin, and he staggered. Then he lowered his head and came around the table like a bull. They wrestled against the table, knocking a Sèvres cup to the floor.

"That's a lie," Carroll whispered. "I've never laid a finger on Felicia . . . on any woman but Helena."

"I've seen Felicia look at you," Hunt panted. His head came up, butting. Carroll fell down.

"John. Meredith."

The wheelchair was in the doorway. Helena was as pale as her husband.

Carroll got to his feet. "Go back, Helena. Go upstairs."

"Meredith. Please leave."

The big lawyer straightened, fumbling his expensive silk tie. He was glaring in a sort of victory. Then he went into the foyer, took his hat and topcoat from the chair in which Mrs. Poole had deposited them, and quietly left.

"John, what did he say to you?" Helena was as close to fear as she ever got. "What happened?"

Carroll began to pick up the fragments of the shattered cup. But his hands were shaking so uncontrollably that he had to stop.

"Oh, darling, you promised never to lose your temper again this way—"

Carroll said nothing.

"It's not good for you." She reached over and pulled his head down to her breast. "Whatever he said, dearest, it's not worth . . ."

He patted her, trying to pull away.

"John, come to bed?"

"No. I've got to cool off."

"Darling—"

"I'll walk it off."

"But it's pouring!"

Carroll snatched his hat and topcoat from the foyer closet and plunged out of the house. He sloshed down Fifth Avenue in the rain and fog, almost running.

The next morning John Carroll got out of the taxi before the Hunt house on East 61st Street like a man in a dream. The streets had been washed clean by the downpour of the night before, and the sun was already hot, but he felt dirty and cold. He pressed the Hunt bell with a sense of doom, a vague warning of horrid things to come he tried not to imagine. He shivered and jabbed the bell again, irritably this time.

A maid with a broad Spanish-Indian face opened the door. She led him in silence up to Felicia Hunt's rooms on the second floor. Tully West was already there, thoughtfully contemplating the postage-stamp rear garden from Felicia's picture window. West was as tall and fleshless as a Franciscan monk, an easy man with an iron-gray crewcut and unnoticeable clothes.

Carroll nodded to West and dropped into one of the capacious Spanish chairs Felicia surrounded herself with. "Crosstown traffic held me up. Felicia, what's this all about?"

Felicia de los Santos Hunt was in her dramatic mood this morning. She had clothed her dark plump beauty in a violently gay gown; she was already fingering her talisman, a ruby-and-emerald-crusted locket that had belonged to a Bourbon queen. Felicia was the daughter of a Latin-American diplomat of Castilian blood; she had been educated in Europe after a high-walled childhood, and she was hopelessly torn between the Spanish tradition of the submissive wife and the feminism she had found in the United States. What Felicia de los Santos had seen in Meredith Hunt, an American primitive twice her age, Carroll had never fathomed.

"Meredith is missing." She had a charming accent.

"Missing? Isn't he in Chicago?"

"The Michaelson people say no." Tully West's witty, rather glacial voice was not amused today. "They phoned Felicia this morning after trying to reach the office. Meredith never got there."

Carroll felt his forehead; he had a jolting headache. "I don't understand. He stopped by last night about half-past nine and said he was on his way to the airport."

"He wasn't on the plane." Hunt's wife seemed more annoyed than alarmed. "Tully just had La Guardia on the phone."

"All planes were grounded from about eight P.M. yesterday until three in the morning by the fog," said West. "Meredith checked in at the field all right, found his flight delayed, and left word at the desk that he'd wait around the airport. But when the fog cleared and the flight was announced they couldn't find him." Carroll's partner sat Felicia Hunt down on her silk divan, handling her gingerly. She appealed to him with her moist black eyes, but he turned to Carroll. "How long did he stay last night, John?"

"When he stopped by? For just a few minutes." Carroll shut his eyes, remembering their tussle. "He didn't mention anything that would explain this."

Felicia Hunt twisted her locket; her perfect teeth glittered. "He's left me."

Tully West looked shocked. "Left you? My dear Felicia! Meredith would as soon leave his wallet."

The maid said from the doorway, urgently, *"Señora. The police."*

Her mistress stiffened. Carroll turned sharply.

Three men were in the doorway behind the Indian woman. One was vast and powerful; one was small, gray and wiry; and the third was tall, slender and young.

The broad man said, "Mrs. Hunt? Sergeant Velie. This is Inspector Queen." He did not bother to introduce the tall young man. "We've got bad news for you."

"My husband—"

"An officer found him around six-thirty this morning on East 58th, near the Queensboro Bridge, in a parked Thunderbird. He was spread across the wheel with a slug in his brain."

She got to her feet, clutching the pendant. Then her eyes turned over and she pitched forward.

West and Carroll both caught her before their mouths could close. They hauled her onto the divan and Carroll began to chafe her hands. The maid ran to the bathroom.

"Ever the delicate touch, Velie," the tall young man remarked from the doorway. "Couldn't you have hit her over the head?"

Sergeant Velie ignored him. "I forgot to mention he's dead. Who are you?"

"I'm Tully West, that's John Carroll." West was very pale. "We're Hunt's partners. Mrs. Hunt phoned us this morning when her husband failed to show up in Chicago for a business appointment. He was to have taken the eleven P.M. plane—"

"That's already been checked." The small gray man was watching the maid wave a bottle of smelling salts under Felicia Hunt's little nose. "Hunt didn't come back home last night? Phone or anything?"

"Mrs. Hunt says not."

"Was he supposed to be traveling alone?"

"Yes."

"Make such trips often?"

"Yes. Hunt was outside man for the firm."

"Was he in the habit of driving his car to airports?"

"Yes. He'd park it and pick it up on his return."

"Carrying any valuables last night?"

"Just cash for the trip, as far as I know. And a dispatch case containing some papers and a change of linen."

Felicia Hunt shuddered and opened her eyes. The maid eased her expertly back on the divan and slipped a pillow under her head. The young widow lay there like Goya's Duchess, picking at her locket. Carroll straightened.

"Suicide," Tully West said, and he cleared his throat. "It was suicide?"

"Not on your tintype," Inspector Queen said. "Hunt was murdered, and when we identify the Colt Woodsman we found in the car, we'll know who murdered him. Until we do, any suggestions?"

Carroll glared around helplessly. Then he clapped his hand over his mouth and ran into Felicia Hunt's bathroom. They heard him gagging.

"Was Mr. Carroll unusually fond of Mr. Hunt?" asked the tall young man politely.

"No," Tully West said. "I mean— Oh, damn it all!"

"Detectives will be talking to you people later in the day." The Inspector nodded at his sergeant, said "Come along, Ellery" to the tall young man, and then he marched out with his old man's stiff-kneed bounce.

"Come in, please." Inspector Queen did not look up from the report he was reading.

John Carroll came into the office between Tully West and a detective. The partners were gray-faced.

"Have a seat."

The detective left. In a rivuleted leather chair at one corner of his father's office Ellery sprawled over a cigaret. A small fan was going behind the old man, ruffling his white hair. It made the only noise in the room.

"See here," Tully West said frigidly. "Mr. Carroll's been interrogated from hell to breakfast by precinct detectives, Homicide Squad men, the deputy chief inspector in charge of Manhattan East, and detectives of the Homicide Bureau. He's submitted without a murmur to fingerprinting. He's spent a whole morning in the Criminal Courts Building being taken apart piece by piece by an assistant district attorney who apparently thinks he can parlay this case into a seat in Congress. May I suggest that you people either fish or cut bait?"

The Inspector laid aside the report. He settled back in his swivel chair, regarding the Ivy League lawyer in a friendly way. "Any special reason, Mr. West, why you insisted on coming along this morning?"

"Why?" West's lips were jammed together. "Is there an objection to my being here?"

"No." The old man looked at Carroll. "Mr. Carroll, I'm throwing away the book on this one. You'll notice there's not even a stenographer present. Maybe if we're frank with each other we can cut corners and save everybody a lot of grief. We've been on this homicide for five days now, and I'm going to tell you what we've come up with."

"But why me?" John Carroll's voice came out all cracked.

West touched his partner's arm. "You'll have to forgive Mr. Carroll, Inspector. He never learned not to look a gift horse in the mouth. Shut up, John, and listen."

The old man swiveled creakily to look out his dusty window. "As far as we can reconstruct the crime, Hunt's killer must have followed him to La Guardia last Friday night. A bit past midnight Hunt reclaimed his car at the parking lot and drove off, in spite of the fact that he'd told the airline clerk at ten-thirty that he'd wait around for the fog to lift. It's our theory that the killer met him at La Guardia and talked him into taking a ride, maybe on a plea of privacy. That would mean that after reclaiming his car Hunt picked the killer up, and they drove off together.

"We have no way of knowing how long they cruised around before crossing the Queensboro Bridge in Manhattan, but at around one forty-five A.M. a patrol car passed the Thunderbird on East 58th, parked where it was later found with Hunt's body in it. The deputy assistant medical examiner says Hunt was killed between two and four A.M. Saturday, so when the patrol car passed at a quarter to two, Hunt and his killer must have been sitting in it, still talking.

"Now." Inspector Queen swiveled back to eye Carroll. "Item one: Hunt was shot to death with a bullet from the Colt Woodsman .22 automatic found beside the body. That pistol, Mr. Carroll, is registered in your name."

Carroll's face went grayer. He made an instinctive clutching movement, but West touched his arm again.

"Item two: motive. There's nothing to indicate it could have had anything to do with Hunt's trip, or any client. Your firm doesn't practice criminal law, your clients are conservative corporations, and the Chicago people had every reason to want Hunt to stay healthy —he was going to save them a couple of million dollars in a tax-refund suit against the government. Mr. West has gone over the contents of Hunt's dispatch case, and he says nothing is missing. Robbery? Hunt's secretary got him three hundred dollars from the bank Friday for his trip, and well over that amount was found in his wallet. Hunt's Movado wristwatch and jade ring were found on him.

"That's the way it stood till Monday morning. Then Hunt himself tipped us off to the motive. He wrote us a letter."

"Hunt *what?*" Carroll croaked.

"By way of Miss Connor, his secretary. She found it in the office mail Monday morning. Hunt wrote it on airline stationery from La Guardia Friday night and dropped it into a mailbox there, probably before his killer showed up.

"It was a note to his secretary," the Inspector went on, "instructing her that if anything should happen to him over the weekend she was to deliver the enclosure, a sealed envelope, to the police. Miss Connor brought it right in."

West said, "Good old Meredith." He looked disgusted.

"Hunt's letter to us, Mr. Carroll, says that he visited your home on Fifth Avenue before going to the airport Friday evening—tells us why, tells us about your fight . . . incidentally clearing up the reason for the bruise on his mouth. So, you see, we know all about the twenty grand you lifted from that trust fund, and Hunt's ultimatum to you a few hours before he was knocked off. He even mentioned his suspicions about you and Mrs. Hunt." The Inspector added mildly, "That's two pretty good motives, Mr. Carroll. Care to change your statement?"

Carroll's mouth was open. Then he jumped up. "It's all a horrible misunderstanding," he stammered. "There's never been a thing between Felicia Hunt and me—"

"John." West pulled him down. "Inspector, Meredith Hunt was stupidly jealous of his wife. He even accused me on occasion of making passes at her. I can't speak about Mrs. Hunt's feelings, but John Carroll is the most devoted married man I know. He's crazy about his wife and children."

"And the defalcation?" the Inspector murmured.

"John's told me all about that. His no-good brother was in serious trouble and John foolishly borrowed the money from one of the trusts our firm administers to get the brute out of it. I've already replaced it from my personal funds. Any talk of theft or prosecution is ridiculous. If I'd known about Meredith's ultimatum I'd have been tempted to pop him one myself. We all have our weak moments under stress. I've known John Carroll intimately for almost ten years. I can and do vouch for his fundamental honesty."

Ellery's voice said from his corner, "And when exactly did Mr. Carroll tell you about his weak moment, Mr. West?"

The lawyer was startled. Then he turned around and said, with a smile, "I don't believe I'll answer that."

"The gun," Inspector Queen prompted.

"It's John's, Inspector, of course. He's a Reserve officer, and he likes to keep up his markmanship. We both do a bit of target-shooting now and then at a gun club we belong to downtown, and John keeps the target pistol in his desk at the office. Anyone could have lifted that Woodsman and walked off with it. The fact that John keeps it in the office is known to dozens of people."

"I see." The old man's tone specified nothing. "Now let's get to last Friday night. We'll play it as if you've never been questioned, Mr. Carroll. I suppose you can establish just where you were between two and four A.M. last Saturday morning?"

Carroll put his head between his hands and laughed.

"Well, can you?"

"I'll try to explain again, Inspector," Carroll said, straightening up. "When I lose my temper, as I did with Meredith Friday night, I get a violent physical reaction. It takes me hours sometimes to calm down. My wife knows this, and after Meredith left for La Guardia she tried to get me to go to bed. I wish to God I had taken her advice! I decided instead to walk it off, and that's just what I did. I must have walked around half the night."

"Meet anyone you know?"

"I've told you. No."

"What time was it when you got back home?"

"I don't remember. All I know is, it was still dark."

"Was it also still foggy?" the voice from the corner said.

Carroll jumped. "No. No, it wasn't."

Ellery said, "The fog lifted about two A.M., Mr. Carroll."

"You're sure you can't recall the time even approximately?" Inspector Queen's tone was patience itself. "I mean the time you got home?"

Carroll began to look stubborn. "I just didn't notice."

"Maybe Mrs. Carroll did?"

"My wife was asleep. I didn't wake her."

"Item three," the Inspector remarked. "No alibi. And item four: fingerprints."

"Fingerprints?" Carroll said feebly.

"John's? Where, Inspector?" Tully West asked in a sharp tone. "You realize they wouldn't mean anything if you found them on the pistol?"

"We hardly ever find fingerprints on automatics, Mr. West. No, in Hunt's car."

Through the roaring in his ears John Carroll thought: So that's why they fingerprinted me Monday . . . He blinked as he heard the old amusement in his partner's voice.

"Surely you found other prints in the car besides John's and, I assume, Hunt's?"

The old man looked interested. "Whose, for instance?"

"There must be at least one set traceable to the attendant in the public garage where Hunt kept his car."

"Well?"

"And, of course," West said with a smile, "a few of mine."

"Yours, Mr. West?"

"I'm afraid I'm going to have to insist that you take my prints, too. Hunt drove John and me home from the office in the Thunderbird Thursday night—the night before the murder."

Inspector Queen snapped, "Of course, Mr. West, we'll oblige you," and glanced over at the leather chair.

"I have a naïve question for you, Carroll." Ellery was studying the smoke-curl of his cigaret. "Did you kill Meredith Hunt?"

"Hell, no," John Carroll said. "I haven't killed anybody since Leyte."

"I think I'm going to advise you not to say any more, John!" Tully West rose. "Is that all, Inspector?"

"For now. And, Mr. Carroll."

"Yes?"

"You're not to leave town. Understand?"

John Carroll nodded slowly. "I guess I do."

Through the lobby of Police Headquarters, down the worn steps to the sidewalk, neither partner said anything. But when they were in a taxi speeding uptown, Carroll kicked the jump-seat and muttered, "Tully, there's something I've got to know."

"What's that?"

"Do you think I murdered Meredith?"

"Not a chance."

"Do you really mean that?"

West's monkish face crinkled. "We Wests haven't stuck our necks out since Great-grandfather West had his head blown off at Chancellorsville."

Carroll sank back. The older man glanced out the cab window at Fourth Avenue.

"On the other hand, you don't lean your weight on a lily pad when a nice big rock is handy. My knowledge of corporation and tax law—or yours, John—isn't going to do much good if that smart old coot decides to jump. You may need a top-flight criminal lawyer soon. To tell the truth, I've been thinking of Sam Rayfield."

"I see. All right, Tully, whatever you say." Carroll studied an inflamed carbuncle on their driver's neck. "Tully, what's the effect of this thing going to be on Helena? And on Breckie, Louanne? My God."

He turned to the other window, lips trembling.

A detective from the 17th Precinct made the arrest that afternoon. He and his partner appeared at the Madison Avenue offices of Hunt, West & Carroll just before five o'clock. Carroll recognized them as the men who had questioned him the previous Saturday afternoon;

they were apparently the local detectives "carrying" the case.

Miss Mallowan fainted out of season. Tully West's secretary dragged her away.

"I'd like to call my wife," Carroll said.

"Sure, but make it snappy."

"Listen, sweetheart," Carroll said into the phone. He was amazed at the steadiness of his voice. "I'm being arrested. You're not to come running down to the Tombs, do you hear? I want you to stay home and take care of the kids. Understand, Helena?"

"You listen to me." Helena's voice was as steady as his. "You're to let Tully handle everything. I'll tell the children you've had to go off on business. And I'll see you as soon as they'll let me. Do *you* understand, darling?"

Carroll licked his lips. "Yes."

Tully West came running out as they waited for the elevator. "I'm getting Rayfield on this right away. And I'll keep an eye on Helena and the brats. You all right, John?"

"Oh, wonderful," Carroll said wryly.

West gripped his hand and dashed off.

The hard gray-and-green face of the Criminal Courts Building, the night in the cell, the march across the bridge from the prison wing the next morning, his arraignment in one of the chill two-story courtrooms, Helena's strained face as she labored up to kiss him, Tully West's droopy look, the soft impressive voice of Samuel Rayfield, the trap of the judge's gray mouth as he fixed bail at fifty thousand dollars . . . to John Carroll, all of it jumbled into an indigestible mass. He was relieved to find himself back in the cell, and he dozed off at once.

Friday morning the pain caught up with him. Everything hurt sharply. When he was taken into the office of the court clerk, he could not bear to look at the two lawyers, or at his wife. He felt as if his clothing had been taken away.

He heard only dimly the colloquy with the clerk. It had something to do with the bail . . . Suddenly Carroll realized that it was his wife who was putting up the bail bond, paying the ransom for his freedom out of Vanowen money.

"Helena, no!"

But he voiced the cry only in his head. The next thing he knew they were marching out of the court clerk's office.

"Am I free?" Carroll asked foolishly.

"You're free, darling," Helena whispered.

"But fifty thousand," he muttered. "Your money . . ."

"Oh, for heaven's sake, John," West said. "The bail is returnable on the first day of the trial, when you resubmit to the custody of the court. You know that."

"John dear, it's only money."

"Helena, I didn't do it . . ."

"I know, darling."

Rayfield interposed his genial bulk between them and the lurking photographers and reporters. Somehow, he got them through the barrage of cameras and questions.

As the elevator doors were closing, Carroll noticed a tall man lounging in the corridor, a youngish man with bright eyes. A shock of recognition, rather unpleasant, ran through him. It was that police inspector's son, Ellery Queen. What was he doing here?

The question needled him all the way home.

Then he was safe behind the gray front on Fifth Avenue. In the Tombs, Carroll had coddled the thought of that safety, wrapping himself in it against the cold steel and antiseptic smell. But they were still with him. When Mrs. Poole took the children tactfully off to the Park, Carroll shivered and gave himself up to the martini West handed him.

"What was it Meredith used to say about your martinis, Tully? Something about having to be a fifth-generation American to know how to mix one properly?"

"Meredith was a middle-class snob." West raised his glass. "Here's to him. May he never know what hit him."

They sipped in silence.

Then Helena set her glass down. "Tully. Just what does Mr. Rayfield think?"

"The trial won't come up until October."

"That's not what I asked."

"Translation," Carroll murmured. "What are defendant's chances?"

"Rayfield hasn't said." West downed the rest of his drink in a gulp, something he never did.

Helena's silky brows drew the slightest bit toward each other. She said suddenly, "John, you have some enemy you don't know about. Someone who hates you enough to commit murder with your gun. Who is it? Think, darling!"

Carroll shook his head.

"I don't believe it's that at all, Helena," West said, pouring a refill. "Taking John's pistol might have been an act of sheer opportunism. Whoever it was might have lifted mine if I'd left it around. Seems to me the question properly is, Who had it in for Meredith?"

"That's junior, remember?" Carroll said. "Ask the police. Ask that lip-smacking little assistant district attorney."

They were all quiet again.

"But it's true," John Carroll mumbled at last. "It's true I've got to do something . . ."

Tully West's eyes met Helena Carroll's briefly.

"Here, John. Have another martini."

Carroll spent the weekend in seclusion. The telephone and doorbell kept ringing, but Helena refused to let him be disturbed.

By Sunday night he had made up his mind. Helena heard him typing away on the portable, but when she tried to go in to him, she found the bedroom door locked.

"John! Are you all right?"

"I'll be out in a minute."

When he unlocked the door he was tucking an envelope into his inside breast pocket. He looked calmer, as if he had won a battle with himself.

He helped her over to the chaise. "There's something I've never told anyone, Helena, not even you. I gave my word not to."

"What are you talking about, darling?"

"I've had a big decision to make. Helena, I'm going to come out of this all right. All I ask you to do is stop worrying and trust me. No matter what happens, will you trust me?"

"Oh, John!"

He stooped to kiss her. "I'll be back in a few minutes."

He walked over to Madison Avenue and went into a deserted delicatessen store. In the telephone booth he dialed Meredith Hunt's number.

"Serafina? Mr. Carroll. Let me talk to Mrs. Hunt."

Felicia Hunt's accent vibrated in his ear without its usual charm. "John, are you mad? Suppose they have my telephone tapped? You know what Meredith wrote them!"

"I also know he got it all cross-eyed," Carroll said. "Felicia, I want to see you. Tomorrow I'm going into the office to start helping Tully salvage something from the wreckage, but on my way home I'm stopping in at your place with somebody about six-thirty. Will you be there?"

She sounded exasperated. "I can't go anywhere so soon after the funeral, you know that. Whom are you bringing?"

"No one you know."

"John, I wish you wouldn't—"

He hung up.

When the maid with the Indian face opened the door Carroll said, "After you, Rudin," and the man with him stepped nervously into the Hunt house. He was a chubby citizen with a wet pink scalp and rimless eyeglasses. He carried a small leather case.

"The *Señora* waits upstairs," Serafina said sullenly.

"Get Mr. Rudin a magazine or something," Carroll said. "This won't take long, Rudin."

The man seated himself on the edge of a foyer chair. Carroll vaulted up the stairs, taking his briefcase with him.

Felicia Hunt was all in black. Even her stockings were black. She gave Carroll a turn; it was rather like walking in on a character drawn by Charles Addams. She wore no make-up and, for the first time since Carroll had known her, no jewelry, not even her pendant. The brilliant fingernails she affected were now colorless. Her fingers kept exploring her bosom petulantly.

"Meaning no disrespect to an old Spanish custom," Carroll said, "is this mourning-in-depth absolutely necessary, Felicia? You look like a ghost."

"Thank you," Felicia said spitefully. "Always the *caballero*. Where I come from, John, you do certain things in certain ways. Not that I would dare show my face in the street! Reporters . . . may they all *rot*! What do you want?"

Carroll set his briefcase down by the escritoire, went to the door, and carefully closed it. She watched him with sudden interest. He glanced about, nodded at the drawn drapes.

"How mysterious," the widow said in a new tone. "Are you going to kill me or kiss me?"

Carroll laughed. "You're a nourishing dish, Felicia, but if I didn't have an appetite for you a year ago I'd hardly be likely to drool over you now."

She flung herself on the divan. "Go away," she said sulkily. "I loathe you."

"Why? Because it took you too long to realize what it would mean to *Señor* the Ambassador, your father, if your passes at me ever got into the newspapers? You didn't loathe me when you were throwing yourself at me all over town, waylaying me in restaurants, making Meredith suspect I was fouling his nest. Have you forgotten those steaming *billets-doux* you kept sending me, Felicia?"

"And how you nobly protected me by saying nothing about them." She spat at him, "Get out!"

"Yes, I protected you," Carroll said slowly, "but it begins to look as if I can't protect you any longer. I've told everyone—the police, the D.A., Helena, Tully, Samuel Rayfield—that I walked the streets in the rain most of the night that Meredith was shot. As far as they're concerned, right now I have no alibi for the two-hour stretch between two and four A.M., when they say he was murdered."

She was beginning to look apprehensive.

"But now I'm afraid I'm going to have to tell them that between one o'clock and four-thirty that morning you and I were alone in this room, Felicia. That the fact is, I've had an alibi all along—you—and that I kept my mouth shut about it because of how it would look if the story came out."

She said hoarsely, "You wouldn't."

"Not if I can help it." Carroll shrugged. "For one thing, I'm quite aware that nobody, not even Helena, would believe I spent three and a half hours alone with you that night just trying to get you to talk Meredith out of ruining my life. Especially if it also came out, as might very well happen, how you'd run after me, written me those uninhibited Latin love letters."

Her white skin turned ghastly.

"They'd jump to the worst possible conclusion about that night. I don't want that any more than you do, Felicia, although for a different reason. A woman in Helena's physical condition never feels very secure about her husband, no matter how faithful he is to her. A yarn like this . . ." Carroll set his jaw. "I love Helena, but I may have no choice. I'm no storybook hero, Felicia. I'm facing the possibility of the electric chair. That alibi is my life-insurance policy. I wouldn't be any good to Helena and the children dead."

"Crucified," Felicia Hunt said bitterly. "I'd be crucified! I won't do it."

"You've got to."

"I won't! You can't make me!"

"If I have to, I will."

Murder glittered from her black eyes. But Carroll did not flinch, and after a moment the glitter flickered and she turned away.

"What do you want me to do?"

"I've typed out a statement. At the moment, all you have to do is sign it. I've brought a man with me to notarize your signature; he's downstairs. He has no idea what kind of document it is. I'll lock it in my safe at the office. Don't look at me that way, Felicia. I've got to protect myself now. You ought to be able to understand that."

She said venomously, "Go call your damned notary," and jumped off the divan.

"You'd better read the statement first."

Carroll took a long manila envelope from his briefcase. It was unsealed, bound with a red rubber band. He removed the rubber band, opened the envelope, and took from it a folded sheet of typewriter paper. He unfolded it and handed it to her.

She read it carefully, twice. Then she laughed and handed it back.

"Pig."

Carroll opened the door, paper in hand. "Mr. Rudin? Would you come up now, please?"

The notary appeared, mopping his pink scalp. In the other hand he clutched the leather case. He sneaked a glance at Felicia's frank figure and immediately looked away.

"This is Mrs. Felicia de los Santos Hunt, widow of the late Meredith Hunt," Carroll said. "Do you need proof of her identity?"

"I've seen Mrs. Hunt's picture in the papers." Rudin

had a pink sort of voice, too. He opened his case and spread out on the escritoire an ink pad, several rubber stamps, and a notary's seal. From his breast pocket he produced a fountain pen as big as a cigar. "Now," he said. "We're all set."

Carroll laid the statement, folded except for the bottom section, on the escritoire. He kept his hand on the fold. Felicia snatched the pen from the notary and signed her name in a vicious scrawl.

When the notary was finished, Carroll slipped the paper into the manila envelope, put the red rubber band around it, and stowed the envelope in his briefcase. He rezipped the case.

"I'll see you out, Rudin."

They passed Serafina on the stairs; she was wiping the banister with a damp cloth and she did not look at them.

In the foyer Carroll gave the little man a ten-dollar bill, relocked the street door behind him, and returned upstairs. Serafina would not give an inch; he had to walk around her.

Her mistress was lying on the divan, also turned away from him. Goya's Duchess, Carroll thought, rear view. He could hear the Indian slamming things around on the stairs.

"Thanks, Felicia." He grinned at the swelling rump. "You've saved my life."

She did not reply.

"I promise I won't use the statement except as a last resort."

When she continued to ignore him, Carroll picked up his briefcase and left.

Carroll surrendered himself to the Court on the morning of the second Monday in October. In the battlefield of TV reporters, photographers, and legmen, through the log-jammed corridor, in the courtroom itself, the only thing he could think of was where the summer had gone. July, August, September seemed never to

have existed. Certainly they did not occupy the same
space-time as the nightmare he found himself in.

The nightmare shuttled fast, a disconnected sequence
of pictures like random frames from a film. The group
face of the panel, one compound jury eye and mouth,
the whispering of shoes, mysterious palavers before the
bench of the black-robed man suspended in midair—
opening statements, questions, answers, gavels, objec-
tions . . . Suddenly it was Wednesday evening and Carroll was back in his cell.

He felt a childish impulse to laugh aloud and choked
it off.

He must have dozed, for the next thing he knew, Tully West was peering down at him as from a great height,
and behind Tully West loomed a familiar figure. Carroll
could not remember the cell door's opening or closing.

He sat up quickly.

"John, you remember Ellery Queen," said West.

Carroll nodded. "You fellows are doing quite a job
on me, Queen."

"Not me," Ellery said. "I'm strictly ground observer
corps."

"One of the few advantages of being in my position is
that a man can be blunt," Carroll said. "What do you
want?"

"Satisfaction," Ellery said. "I'm not getting it."

Carroll glanced at his partner. "What's this, Tully?"

"Queen came to me after the session today and ex-
pressed interest in your case." West managed a smile.
"It struck me, John, this might be a nice time to encour-
age him."

Carroll rested his head against the cell wall. For days
part of his mind had been projecting itself into the execution chamber at Sing Sing, and another part had
counterattacked with thoughts of Helena and Breckie
and Louanne. He took Helena and the children to sleep
with him for sheer self-preservation.

"What is it you're not satisfied about?"

"That you shot Hunt."

"Thanks," Carroll said and laughed. "Too bad you're not on the jury."

"Yes," Ellery said. "But then I don't have the respectful jury mind. I'm not saying you didn't shoot Hunt; I'm just not convinced. Something about this case has bothered me from the start. Something about you, in fact. I wish you'd clear it up, if not for my sake then for yours. It's later than you apparently think."

Carroll said very carefully, "How bad is it?"

"As bad as it can be."

"I've told Queen the whole story, John." West's urbanity was gone; he even did a little semaphore work with his long arms. "And I may as well tell you that Rayfield holds out very little hope. He says today's testimony of the night man at the office building was very damaging."

"How could it be?" Carroll cried. "He admitted himself he couldn't positively identify as me whoever it was he let into the building that night. It wasn't me, Tully. It was somebody who deliberately tried to look like me— coat and hat like mine, my stumpy walk from that leg wound on Leyte, easily imitated things like that. And then the guy lets himself into our office and swipes my gun. I should think even a child would see I'm being had!"

"Where would a stranger get a key to your office?" Ellery asked.

"How do I know? How do I know he was even a stranger?"

After a while Carroll became conscious of the silence. He looked up angrily.

"You don't believe me. Actually, neither of you believes me."

West said, "It's not that, John," unhappily, and began to pace off the cell.

"Look," Ellery said. "West tells me you've hinted at certain important information that for some unimaginable reason you've been holding back. If it can do anything to clear you, Carroll, I'd advise you to toss it into the pot right now."

A prisoner shouted somewhere. West stopped in his tracks. Carroll put his head between his hands.

"I did something that Friday night that can clear me, yes."

"What!" West cried.

"But it's open to all sorts of misinterpretation, chiefly nasty."

"Nastier than the execution chamber at Sing Sing?" Ellery murmured.

West said, "A woman," with a remote distaste.

"That's right, Tully." Carroll did not look at Ellery, feeling vaguely offended at his indelicacy. "And I promised her I wouldn't use this except as a last resort. It wasn't for her sake, God knows. I've kept my mouth shut because of Helena. Helena loves me, but she's a woman, and a sick woman at that. If she shouldn't believe me . . ."

"Let me get this straight," Ellery said. "You were with this other woman during the murder period? You can prove an alibi?"

"Yes."

"And he keeps quiet about it!" West dropped to the steel bunk beside his friend. "John, how many kinds of idiot are you? Don't you have any faith in Helena at all? What happened? Who's the woman?"

"Felicia."

"Oh," West said.

"Mrs. Hunt?" Ellery said sharply.

"That's right. I wandered around in the rain that night trying to figure out how I was going to stop Meredith from disclosing that twenty-thousand-dollar lunacy and having me arrested. That's when I thought of Felicia. She'd always been able to get anything out of Meredith that she wanted. I phoned her from a pay station and asked if I couldn't come right over . . . I was pretty panicky, I guess . . ." His voice petered out.

"Well, well?" West muttered.

"She was still up, reading in bed. When I told her what it was about, she said to come. She let me in herself. The maid was asleep, I suppose—anyway, I didn't see Serafina."

"And the time?" Ellery demanded.

"It was just about one A.M. when I got there. I left at four-thirty." Carroll laughed. "Now you know why I've kept quiet about this. Can I expect my wife to believe that I spent three and a half hours in the middle of the night alone with Felicia in her bedroom—and she in a sheer nightgown and peekaboo negligee, by God!—just talking? And not getting anywhere, I might add."

"Three and a half hours?" Ellery's brows were way up.

"Felicia didn't see any reason why she should save my neck. Charming character." Carroll's shoulders sloped. "Well, I told you what it would sound like. I'm sure I'd doubt the story myself."

"How much of the time did you have to fight for your honor?" West murmured. "If I didn't know John so well, Queen, I'd be skeptical, too. Felicia's had a mad thing for him. But he's always been allergic to her. I suppose, John, she was willing to make a deal that night?"

"Something like that."

"One night of amour in return for her influence on dear Meredith in your behalf. Yes, that would be Felicia's steamy little libido at work. But Helena . . ." West frowned. "Quite a situation at that."

Ellery said, "It will have to be risked. Carroll, will Mrs. Hunt support your alibi in court?"

"She'd find it pretty tough to deny her own signature. I had her sign a full statement before a notary."

"Good. Where is the statement?"

"In my safe at the office. It's in a plain manila evenlope, marked 'Confidential' and bound around with a red rubber band."

"I suggest you give West permission to open your safe, and I'd like to go along as security. Right now."

Carroll bit his lip. Then, abruptly, he nodded.

"Do you know the combination, West?"

"Unless John's changed it. It's one of those letter-combination safes in which you can make the combination any word you want. John, is the combination word still 'Helena'?"

"No. I've changed the damn thing four times this summer. The word is now 'rescue.' "

"And that," West said solemnly, "is sheer poetry. Well, John, if the open-sesame Queen lugs around in his wallet should work again in this Bastille, we'll be back here shortly."

They were as good as West's word. Less than ninety minutes later the guard readmitted them to Carroll's cell. Ellery had the manila envelope in his hand. He tossed the envelope to the bunk.

"All right, Carroll, let's hear it."

"You haven't opened it?"

"I'd rather you did that yourself."

Carroll picked up the envelope. He slipped the red rubber band off and around his wrist and, with an effort, inserted his fingers into the envelope.

West said, "John. What's the matter?"

"Is this a gag?" Carroll's fingers kept clawing around in the envelope.

"Gag?"

"It's empty! The statement's not here!"

Ellery looked interested. He took the envelope from Carroll's frantic hand, squeezed it open, and peered inside. "When did you see the contents last?"

"I opened the safe several times this summer to make sure the envelope was still there, but I never thought to examine it. I just took it for granted . . ." Carroll sprang from the bunk. "Nobody could have got into that safe—nobody! Not even my secretary. Nobody knew the combination words!"

"John, John." West was shaking him.

"But how in God's name . . . Unless the safe was broken into! Was it broken into, Queen?"

"No sign of it."

"Then I don't understand!"

"One thing at a time." Ellery took his other arm and they got him back on the bunk. "The loss isn't necessarily fatal, Carroll. All you have to do is make sure Mrs. Hunt takes the stand and repeats her statement under oath. She'd have been called to testify, anyway, once the written statement had been placed in evidence. Isn't that right, West?"

"Yes. I'll get hold of Felicia right off."

Carroll was gnawing his fingernails. "Maybe she won't agree, Tully. Maybe . . ."

"She'll agree." West sounded grim. "Queen, would you come with me? This is one interview I prefer an unbiased witness for. Keep your shirt on, John."

They were back in Carroll's cell with the first grays of dawn. Carroll, who had dropped off to sleep, sat up stupidly. Then he jerked wide awake. His partner's monkish flesh had acquired a flabbiness he had never seen before. Carroll's glance darted to the tall shadow in the corner of the cell.

"What's the matter now?" Carroll chattered. "What's happened?"

"I'm afraid the absolute worst." Ellery's voice was deeply troubled. "The Hunt house is closed down, Carroll. I'm sorry. Felicia Hunt seems to have disappeared."

That was a bad time for John Carroll. Ellery and West had to do some hard, fast talking to keep him from going to pieces altogether. They talked and talked through the brightening gloom and the tinny sounds of the prison coming to life.

"Hopeless. It's hopeless," Carroll kept muttering.

"No," Ellery said. "Nothing is hopeless. It only looks that way, Carroll. The Fancy Dan who weaves an elaborate shroud for somebody else usually winds up occupying it himself. The clever boys trip over their own cleverness. There's a complex pattern here, and it's getting more tangled by the hour. That's good, Carroll. It's not hopeless at all."

But Carroll only shook his head.

West was striding about the cell. "On the other hand, Queen, let's face the facts. John's lost his alibi. The only thing that could surely save him."

"Temporarily."

"We've got to get that alibi back!"

"I agree. Stop running around in circles, West, you're making me nervous." West stopped in his tracks. "Thank you. For both of us. The obvious step is to find that woman.

"Of course." West looked helpless. "But where do I start? Will you help, Queen?"

Ellery smiled. "I've been hoping you'd ask me that. I'll be glad to, if Carroll wants me."

The man on the bunk roused himself. "Want you? Right now I'd take the devil himself! The question is, What can you do?"

"This and that. Here, have a smoke." Ellery jabbed a cigaret between Carroll's swollen lips. "West, you look beat. How about going home and getting some sleep? Oh, and give my father a ring at home, will you? Tell him about this Felicia Hunt development and ask him for me to hop right to it."

When West had gone, Ellery seated himself on the bunk. For a moment he watched Carroll smoke. Then he said, "Carroll."

"What?"

"Carroll, stop feeling sorry for yourself and listen to me. First, let's try to track down that business of the missing alibi statement. Go back to the time when you approached Felicia to sign it. Where did the meeting take place? When? Give me every fact you can remember, and then dig for some you've left out."

He listened closely. When Carroll was finished, Ellery nodded.

"It's about as I figured. After the Hunt woman signed the statement and Rudin notarized her signature and left, you left with the envelope in your briefcase and instead of going on home returned to your office. You never once, you say, let go of the briefcase. In the office you placed the envelope in your safe without checking its contents, locked the safe, and adjusted the dial to a new combination word. And on the three or four subsequent occasions when you checked on the envelope, you claim nobody could have removed the statement from it while you had the safe open, or discovered the new combinations you kept setting.

"When the envelope did finally leave the safe, the only hands not your own to touch it were mine, last night. And I'll vouch for the fact that the statement couldn't have been stolen from me or lost from the envelope on the way over here." Ellery tapped the manila envelope still in Carroll's slack hand. "So this was empty when I took it from the safe. Carroll, it's been empty for months. It was empty before you ever put it in the safe."

Carroll looked at it, dazed.

"Only one conclusion is possible." Ellery lit another cigaret for him, and one for himself. "The only time the envelope was not actually in your physical possession, or in the safe, or in my hands, was for a couple of minutes in the Hunt house the night Felicia signed the statement. You say that, after she signed and Rudin notarized her signature, you slipped the statement into the envelope and the envelope into your briefcase, that you then took Rudin downstairs to pay him off and see him out. During that couple of minutes the briefcase with its contents were out of your sight and control. Therefore that's when the great disappearance took place. And since Mrs. Hunt was the only one in the room with the briefcase . . ."

"Felicia?"

"Nobody else. Why should she have swiped the statement she had just signed, Carroll? Any idea?"

"She double-crossed me, damn her," Carroll said in a

thick voice. "And now she's ducked out to avoid having to tell the story under oath!"

"Well get her to duck right back in if we have to extradite her from Little America." Ellery rose and squeezed Carroll's shoulder. "Hang on, Johnny."

Felicia Hunt's whereabouts remained a mystery for as long as it took Ellery to go from the Tombs to Police Headquarters. His father had just come into the office and the old man was elbow-deep in reports.

"Yes, West phoned me," the Inspector said without looking up. "If he'd hung on, I'd have been able to tell him in three minutes where Felicia Hunt is. Blast it all, where's that Grierson affidavit?"

Ellery waited patiently for the crisis to pass.

"Well?" he said at last. "I'm cliff-hanging."

"What? Oh!" Inspector Queen leaned back. "All I did was phone Smallhauser at the D.A.'s office. It seems a couple of days before Carroll's trial started—last Saturday morning—Hunt's widow showed up at the D.A.'s all tricked out in that ghastly mourning she wears, with her doctor in tow. The doctor told Smallhauser Mrs. Hunt was in a dangerously nervous state and couldn't face the ordeal of the trial. He wanted her to get away from the city. Seems she'd bought a cottage up in northern Westchester this summer and a few days up there by herself were just what the M.D. ordered, and was it all right with the D.A.? Well, Smallhauser didn't like it, but he figured that with the cottage having a phone he could always get her back to town in a couple of hours. So he said okay, and she gave her maid a week off and went up there Saturday afternoon. What's the hassle?"

Ellery told him. His father listened suspiciously.

"So that's what West was being so mysterious about," he exclaimed. "An alibi! The D.A.'s going to love this."

"So will Rayfield. He doesn't know about it yet, either."

The Inspector cocked a sharpening eye. "What's your stake in this pot?"

"The right," Ellery said piously. "And seeing that it prevails."

His father grunted and reached for the telephone. When he set it down, he had a Mt. Kisco number scribbled on his pad.

"Here, you call her," he said. "I'm working the other side of the street. And don't use a city phone for a toll call! You know where to find a booth."

Ellery was back before his father's desk in forty-five minutes.

"What now?" Inspector Queen said. "I was just on my way to the Bullpen."

"She doesn't answer."

"Who doesn't answer?"

"The Hunt lady," Ellery said. "Remember the case? I've phoned at five-minute intervals for the better part of an hour. Either she's gone into an early hibernation, or she's back in Central America charming the hidalgos."

"Or she just isn't answering her phone. Look, son, I'm up to my lowers this morning. The case is out of my hands, anyway. Keep calling. She'll answer sooner or later."

Ellery tried all day, slipping in and out of the courtroom every half hour. At a little past three the assistant district attorney rested his case, and on the request of the defense, Judge Holloway adjourned the trial until the next morning.

Ellery managed to be looking elsewhere when John Carroll was taken from the courtroom. Carroll walked as if his knees were about to give way. But as the room cleared, Ellery caught Tully West's eye. West, who was stooping over Helena Carroll in distress, nodded and after a moment came over.

"What about Felicia? She'll testify, won't she?" West sounded urgent.

Ellery glanced over at the reporters surrounding the

portly figure of Rayfield. Some were glancing back, noses in the wind.

"We can't talk here, West. Can you get away?"

"I'll have to take Helena home first." West was braced, as if for a blow. "Where?"

"My father's office as soon as you can make it."

"What about Rayfield?"

"Better not say anything to him those newsmen can overhear. We can get in touch with him tonight."

It was nearly five o'clock before the tall lawyer hurried into the Inspector's office. He looked haunted.

"Sorry, Helena went to pieces on me. I had to tell her all about John's alibi. Now she's more confused than ever. Damn it, why didn't John trust her in the first place?" West wiped his face. He said slowly, "And now I suppose you'll tell me Felicia refuses to co-operate."

"I almost wish that were it." Ellery was looking harried himself. "West, I've been phoning since eight-thirty this morning. I tried again only ten minutes ago. Mrs. Hunt doesn't answer."

"She isn't there?"

"Maybe." Inspector Queen was looking annoyed. "Ellery, why the devil won't you ask the help of the State Police? We could have a report on her in an hour."

"No." Ellery got up. "West, do you have your car?"

"I cabbed down."

Ellery glanced at his father. The old man threw up his hands and stamped out.

"I ought to have my head examined! Velie, get me a car."

They drove out of the city on Saw Mill River Parkway, Sergeant Velie at the wheel and Inspector Queen in the suicide seat nursing his grouch. Behind them, from opposite windows, Ellery and West studied the scenery. They were studying it long after darkness fell.

The sergeant turned the unmarked squad car off the Parkway near Mt. Kisco.

"Pull up at that gas station." They were the first words the Inspector had uttered since leaving the city.

"Stony Ride Road?" the attendant said. "That's up between here and Bedford Hills. Dirt job that goes way off to hell and gone. Who you looking for?"

"The Hunt place."

"Hunt? Never heard."

Ellery stuck his head out. "How about Santos?"

"Santos. Yeah, dame of that name bought the old Meeker place this summer. You follow along here about a mile and a half . . ."

"Using her maiden name," West said as they drove away. "Meredith would have loved that."

The Queens said nothing.

Stony Ride Road climbed and twisted and swooped back, jolting their teeth. The darkness was impressive. They saw only two houses in three miles. A mile beyond the second, they found Felicia Hunt's cottage. Sergeant Velie very nearly drove past it; its windows were as black as the night itself.

Velie swung the car between two mossy pillars into a crushed-stone driveway.

"No, Velie, stop here and shine your brights dead on the house." The Inspector sounded troubled.

"She's gone," West growled. "She's gone or she never came here at all! What am I going to tell John?"

Ellery borrowed the sergeant's flash and got out. The Inspector put his small hand on Tully West's arm.

"No, Mr. West, we'll wait here." Trouble was in his look, too.

It was a verdigrised fieldstone cottage with rusty wood trim and a darkly shingled roof, cuddled against wild woods. Ellery played his flash on the door. They saw him extend his foot and toe the door, and they saw it swing back.

He went into the house, flash first. A moment later the hall lit up.

He was in the house exactly two minutes.

At the sight of his face Inspector Queen and Sergeant

Velie jumped from the car and ran past him and into the cottage.

Ellery said, "You can tell John to forget his alibi, West. She's in there dead."

Felicia Hunt was lying on the bedroom floor face down, which was unfortunate, for the back of her head had been crushed. The bloody shards of the heavy stoneware vase that had crushed it strewed the floor around her. In the debris were some stiff chrysanthemums, looking like big dead insects. One of them had fallen on her open right palm.

West swallowed and retreated rapidly to the hall.

She had been dressed in a rainbow-striped frock of some iridescent material when death caught her. Jewels glittered on her hands and arms and neck. There were pomponed scuffs on her feet, her legs were bare, and the dead lips and cheeks and eyes showed no trace of make-up.

"She's been dead at least four days, maybe five," Inspector Queen said. "What do you make of it, Velie?"

"Nearer four," the big sergeant said. "Last Sunday some time, Inspector." He glanced with longing at the tightly closed windows.

"Better not, Velie."

The two men rose. They had touched nothing but the body, and that with profound care.

Ellery stood watching them morosely.

"Find anything, son?"

"No. That rain the other night wiped out any tire tracks or footprints that might have been left. Some spoiling food in the refrigerator, and her car is nicely in the garage behind the house. No sign of robbery." Ellery added suddenly, "Doesn't something about her strike you as queer?"

"Yeah," Sergeant Velie said. "That posy in her hand ought to be a lily."

"Spare us, Velie! What, Ellery?"

"The way she's dressed."

They stared down at her. Tully West came back to the doorway, still swallowing.

The sergeant said, "Looks like she was expecting somebody, the way she's all dolled up."

"That's just what it doesn't look like," Inspector Queen snapped. "A woman as formally brought up as this one, who's expecting somebody, puts on shoes and stockings, Velie—doesn't go around barelegged and wearing bedroom slippers. She hadn't even made up her face or polished her nails. She was expecting nobody. What about the way she's dressed, Ellery?"

"Why isn't she still in mourning?"

"Huh?"

"She drives up here alone Saturday after wearing nothing but unrelieved black in town, and within twenty-four hours or less she's in a color-happy dress, back wearing her favorite jewelry, and having a ball for herself. It tells a great deal about Felicia de los Santos Hunt."

"It doesn't tell me a thing," his father retorted. "What I want to know is why she was knocked off. It wasn't robbery. And there's nothing to indicate rape, although it's true a would-be rapist might have panicked—"

"Isn't it obvious that this is part and parcel of Hunt's murder and the frame-up of John Carroll?" West broke in with bitterness. "Rape! Felicia was murdered to keep her from giving John the alibi that would get him off the hook."

The Inspector nibbled his mustache.

"What does it take to convince you people that somebody is after Carroll's hide!"

"That sounds like sense, Dad."

"Maybe."

"At the least, the Hunt woman's murder is bound to give the case against Carroll a different look— Dad, before Velie phones the State Police."

"Well?"

"Let's you and Velie and I really give this place a going over."

"What for, Ellery?"

"For that alibi statement Felicia signed and then took back when Carroll wasn't looking. It's a long shot, but . . . who knows?"

Their session with the State Police took the rest of the night. It was sunrise before they got back to the city.

West asked to be dropped off at Beekman Place.

"Sam Rayfield won't thank me for waking him up, but then I haven't had any sleep at all. Who's going to tell John?"

"I will," Ellery said.

"West turned away with a grateful wave.

"So far so bad," the Inspector said as they sped downtown. "Now all I have to do is talk the D.A.'s office into joining Rayfield in a plea to Judge Holloway, and why *I* should have to do it is beyond me!"

"You going home, Inspector?"

"Sure I'm going home, Velie! I can take Smallhauser's abuse over my own phone as well as at Headquarters. And maybe get some sleep, too. How about you, son?"

"The Tombs," Ellery said.

He parted with Sergeant Velie at the Headquarters garage and walked over to the Criminal Courts Building. His head was muddy, and he wanted to cleanse it. He tried not to think of John Carroll.

Carroll woke up instantly at the sound of the cell door.

"Queen! How did you make out with Felicia?"

Ellery said, "We didn't."

"She won't testify?"

"She can't testify, John. She's dead."

It was brutal, but he knew no kinder formula. Carroll was half sitting up, leaning on an elbow, and he remained that way. His eyes kept blinking in a monotonous rhythm.

"Dead . . ."

"Murdered. We found her on the bedroom floor of

her cottage with her head smashed in. She'd been dead for days."

"Murdered." Carroll blinked and blinked. "But who—?"

"There's not a clue. So far, anyway." Ellery lit a cigaret and held it out. Carroll took it. But then he dropped it and covered his face with both hands. "I'm sorry, John."

Carroll's hands came down. He had his lower lip in his teeth.

"I'm no coward, Queen. I faced death a hundred times in the Pacific and didn't chicken out. But a man likes to die for some purpose . . . I'm scared."

Ellery looked away.

"There's got to be some way out of this!" Carroll dropped off the bunk and ran in his bare feet to the bars of the cell, to grasp them with both hands. But then he whirled and sprang at Ellery, seizing him by the arms. "That statement, that's my out, Queen! Maybe she didn't destroy it. Maybe she took it up there with her. If you can find it for me—"

"I've looked," Ellery said gently. "And my father looked, and Sergeant Velie, too. We covered the cottage inside and out. It took us over two hours. We didn't call the local police until we were satisfied it wasn't there."

"But it's *got* to be there! My life depends on it! Don't you see?" He shook Ellery.

"Yes, John."

"You missed it. Maybe she put it in an obvious place, like in that story of Poe's. Did you look in her purse? Her luggage?"

"Yes, John."

"Her suits—coats—the linings—?"

"Yes, John."

"Her car?"

"Her car, too."

"Maybe it was on her," Carroll said feverishly. "On her person. Did you—? No, I suppose you wouldn't."

"We would and we did." Ellery's arms ached. He wished Carroll would let go.

"How about that big ruby-and-emerald pendant she was so hipped on? The alibi statement was only a single sheet of paper. She might have wadded it up and hidden it in the locket part. Did you look there while you were searching the body?"

"Yes, John. All we found in the locket were two photos, Spanish-looking elderly people. Her parents, I suppose."

Carroll released him. Ellery rubbed his arms.

"How about books?" Carroll mumbled. "Felicia was always reading some trashy novel or other. She might have slipped it between two pages—"

"There were eleven books in the house, seven magazines. I went through them myself."

In the cold cell Carroll wiped the perspiration from his cheeks.

"Desk with a false compartment? . . . Cellar? . . . Is there an attic? . . . Did you search the garage?"

He went on and on. Ellery waited for him to run down.

When Carroll was finally quiet, Ellery called the guard. His last glimpse of the young lawyer was of a spread-eagled figure, motionless on the bunk, eyes shut. All Ellery could think of was a corpse.

Judge Joseph N. Holloway shook his head. He was a gray-skinned, frozen-eyed veteran of the criminal courts, known to practicing members of the New York bar as Old Steelguts.

"I didn't come down to my chambers an hour early on a Monday morning, Counselor Rayfield, for the pleasure of listening to your mellifluous voice. That pleasure palled on me a long time ago. I granted an adjournment Friday morning because of the Hunt woman's murder, but do you have any evidence to warrant a further postponement? So far I've heard nothing but a lot of booshwah."

Assistant District Attorney Smallhauser nodded admiringly. Judge Holloway's fondness for the slang of his youth—indulged in only *in camera,* of course—was trifled with at the peril of the trifler. "Booshwah is *le mot juste* for it, Your Honor. I apologize for being a party to this frivolous waste of your time."

Samuel Rayfield favored the murderous little assistant D.A. with a head-shrinking glance and clamped his teeth more firmly about his cold cigar. "Come off it, Joe," he said to Judge Holloway. "This is a man's life we're playing footsie with. We're not privileged to kick him to death simply because he acted like a damn fool in holding back his alibi. All I want this adjournment for is time to look for that alibi statement the Hunt woman signed when she was alive enough to write."

Judge Holloway's dentures gleamed toward Smallhauser.

"The alibi statement your client *says* the Hunt woman signed," the little D.A. said with his prim smile.

The Judge's dentures promptly turned to Rayfield.

"I've got the notary, Rudin, to attest to the fact that she signed it," the portly lawyer snapped.

"That she signed some paper, yes. But you people admit yourselves that Carroll concealed the text of the paper from Rudin. For all Rudin knows he might have been notarizing the woman's signature to the lease of a new dog house." The little D.A. turned his smile on the Judge. "I'm bound to say, Your Honor, this whole thing smells more and more to me like a stall."

"Come around some time when you've put on long pants and I'll show you what a real stall smells like, Smallhauser!" the famous lawyer said. "Joe, I'm not stalling. There's a chance she didn't destroy the statement. Not much of one, I admit, but I wouldn't sleep nights if I thought I hadn't exhausted every avenue of investigation in Carroll's behalf."

"You wouldn't lose half of a strangled snore," the Judge said with enjoyment. "Look, Sam, it's all conjecture, and you know it. You can't even show that Mrs.

Hunt stole that alleged statement of hers from Carroll in the first place."

"Ellery Queen showed—"

"I know what Ellery Queen showed. He showed his usual talent for making something out of nothing. Ellery's idea of proof!" The old jurist snorted. "And even if the Hunt woman did steal an alibi statement from Carroll, what did she steal it for if not to flush it down a toilet? And even if she held on to it, where is it? The Queens didn't find it in her Westchester cottage. You ransacked her New York house over the weekend. You got a court order to examine her safe deposit box. You questioned her maid and the people in Carroll's office and God knows whom else, without result. Be reasonable, Sam. That alibi statement either never existed or, if it did, it doesn't exist any more. I can't predicate a postponement on the defendant's unsupported allegation of alibi."

"Of course, if you'd like to put Carroll on the stand," Smallhauser said with a grin, "so I can cross-examine him—

Rayfield ignored him. "All right, Joe. But you can't deny that Hunt's wife has also been murdered. That's a fact in evidence of which we can produce a corpse. And I don't believe in coincidences. When a man's murder is followed by his wife's murder, I say the two are connected. The connection in this case is obvious. The murder of Felicia Hunt was committed in order to blow up Carroll's alibi for the murder of Meredith Hunt and cement Carroll's conviction. How can his trial proceed with this area unexplored? I tell you, Joe, this man is being framed by somebody who's committed two murders in order to pull the frame off! Give us time to explore."

"I remember once sitting here listening to Ellery Queen," Judge Holloway said, exploring his denture for a breakfast tidbit. "You're beginning to sound like his echo. Sam, evidence is what trials are ruled by, and evidence is what you ain't got. Motion denied. My courtroom, gentlemen, ten o'clock on the nose."

Ellery got the answer that Thursday afternoon in the half-empty courtroom while the jury was out deliberating John Carroll's fate.

It came to him after an agonizing reappraisal of the facts as he knew them. He had gone over them times without number before. This time, in the lightning flash he had begun to think would never strike again, he saw it.

By good luck, at the time it came he was alone. Carroll had been taken back to the Tombs, and his wife and the two lawyers had gone with him so that he would not have to sweat out the waiting alone.

A sickish feeling invaded Ellery's stomach. He got up and went out and found the nearest men's room.

When he returned to the courtroom, Tully West was waiting for him.

"Helena wants to talk to you." West's face was green, too.

"No."

"I beg your pardon?"

Ellery shook his head clear. "I mean—yes, of course."

West misunderstood. "I don't blame you. I wish I were anywhere else myself. Rayfield was smart—he bowed out for 'coffee.' "

Carroll was being held in a detention room under guard. Ellery was surprised at his calm, even gentle, look. It was Helena Carroll's eyes that were wild. He was holding her hands, trying to console her.

"Honey, honey, it's going to come out all right. They won't convict an innocent man."

"Why are they taking so *long*? They've been out five hours!"

"That's a good sign, Helena," West said. "The longer they take, the better John's chances are."

She saw Ellery then, and she struggled to her feet and was at him so swiftly that he almost stepped back.

"I thought you were supposed to be so marvelous at these things! You haven't done anything for John— anything."

Carroll tried to draw her back, but she shook him off. Her pain-etched face was livid.

"I don't care, John! You should have hired a real detective while there was still time. I wanted you to—I *begged* you and Tully not to rely on somebody so close to the police!"

"Helena, really." West was embarrassed.

Ellery said stonily, "No, Mrs. Carroll is quite right. I was the wrong man for this, although not for the reason you give, Mrs. Carroll. I wish I had never got mixed up in it."

She was staring at him intently. "That almost sounds as if . . ."

"As if what, Helena?" West was trying to humor her, get her away.

"As if he knows. *Tully, he does.* Look at his face!" She clawed at Ellery. "You know, and you won't say anything! You talk, do you hear? Tell me! *Who's behind this?*"

West was flabbergasted. With surprise John Carroll studied Ellery's face for a moment, then he went to the barred window and stood there rigidly.

"Who?" His wife was weeping now. "Who?"

But Ellery was as rigid as Carroll. "I'm sorry, Mrs. Carroll. I can't save your husband. It's too late."

"Too late," she said hysterically. "How can you say it's too late when—"

"Helena." West took the little woman by the arms and forcibly sat her down. Then he turned to Ellery, his lean face dark. "What's this all about, Queen? You sound as if you're covering up for someone. Are you?"

Ellery glanced past the angry lawyer to the motionless man at the window."

"I'll leave it up to John," he said. "Shall I answer him, John?"

For a moment it seemed as if Carroll had not heard. But then he turned, and there was something about him —a dignity, a finality—that quieted Tully West and

Helena Carroll and sent their glances seeking each other.

Carroll replied clearly, *"No."*

Looking out over the prison yard from the Warden's office, Ellery thought he had never seen a lovelier spring night sky, or a sadder one. A man should die on a stormy night, with all Nature protesting. This, he thought, is cruel and unusual punishment.

He glanced at the Warden's clock.

Carroll had fourteen minutes of life left.

The Warden's door opened and closed behind him. Ellery did not turn around. He thought he knew who it was. He had been half expecting his father for an hour.

"Ellery. I looked for you at the Death House."

"I was down there before, Dad. Had a long talk with Carroll. I thought you'd be here long ago."

"I wasn't intending to come at all. It isn't my business. I did my part of it. Or maybe that's why I'm here. After a lifetime of this sort of thing, I'm still not hardened to it . . . Ellery."

"Yes, Dad."

"Its Helena Carroll. She's hounded and haunted me. She's waiting in an Ossining bar right now with West. I drove them up. Mrs. Carroll thinks I have some drag with you. Do I?"

Ellery said from the window, "In practically everything, Dad. But not in this."

"I don't understand you," the Inspector said heavily. "If you have information that would save Carroll, how can you keep buttoned up now—here? All right, you saw something we didn't. Is it my job you're worried about, because I helped put Carroll on this spot? If you know something that proves his innocence, Ellery, the hell with me."

"I'm not thinking of you."

"Then you can only be thinking of Carroll. He's protecting somebody, he's willing to go to the Chair for it, and you're helping him do it. Ellery, you can't do that."

The old man clutched his arm. "There's still a few minutes. The Warden's got an open line to the Governor's office."

But Ellery shook his head.

Inspector Queen stared at his son's set profile for a moment. Then he went over to a chair and sat down, and father and son waited.

At 11:04 the lights suddenly dimmed.

Both men stiffened.

The office brightened.

At 11:07 it happened again.

And again at 11:12.

After that, there was no change. Ellery turned away from the window, fumbling for his cigarets.

"Do you have a light, Dad?"

The old man struck a match for him. Ellery nodded and sat down beside him.

"Who's going to tell her?" his father said suddenly.

"You are," Ellery said. "I can't."

Inspector Queen rose. "Live and learn," he said.

"Dad—"

The door interrupted them. Ellery got to his feet. The Warden's face was as haggard as theirs. He was wiping it with a damp handkerchief.

"I never get used to it," he said, "never . . . He went very peacefully. No trouble at all."

Ellery said, "He would."

"He gave me a message for you, by the way."

"Thanking him, I suppose," Inspector Queen said bitterly.

"Why yes, Inspector," the Warden said. "He said to tell your son how grateful he was. What on earth did he mean?"

"Don't ask *him*," the Inspector said. "My son's constituted himself a one-man subcommittee of the Almighty. Where you going to wait for me, Ellery?" he demanded as they left the Warden's office. "I mean while I do the dirty work?"

Ellery said stiffly, "Take Helena Carroll and Tully West back to the city first."

"Just tell me one thing. What was Carroll 'grateful' to you for? Who'd you help him cover up?"

But Ellery shook his head. "I'll see you at home afterward."

"Well?" the old man said. He had got into his frayed bathrobe and slippers, and he was nursing a cup of stale coffee with his puffy hands. He looked exhausted. "And it had better be good."

"Oh, it's good," Ellery said. "If good is the word." He had not undressed, had not even removed his topcoat. He sat there as he had come in from the long drive to wait for his father. He stared at the blank Queen wall. "It was a slip of the tongue. I remembered it. After a long time of not remembering. It wouldn't have made any difference if the slip had never been made, or if I'd forgotten it altogether. Any difference to Carroll, I mean. He was sunk from the start. I couldn't save him, Dad. There was nothing to save him on or for. He'd had it."

"What slip?" the old man demanded. "Of whose tongue? Or was I deaf as well as blind?"

"I was the only one who had heard it. It had to do with Felicia Hunt. Her husband dies and she goes into Spanish mourning, total and unadorned. But when she gets off by herself in the hillside cottage, back on go the gay clothes and her favorite jewelry. By herself, mind you—alone. Safe from all eyes, even her maid's."

Ellery stared harder at the wall. "When we got back to town after finding her body, I went directly to the Tombs to tell Carroll about the murder in Westchester of the only human being who could support his alibi. Carroll was frantic. His mind went back to the alibi statement she had signed and retrieved from his briefcase, unknown to him at the time. It was all he could think of, naturally. If that piece of paper existed, if she had hidden it instead of destroying it, he might still be saved. He kept pounding at me. Maybe she'd hidden it in her luggage, her car, a secret drawer. He went on and on. And one of the places he mentioned as a possible hiding place of the statement was the locket of the ruby-and-emerald pendant Felicia Hunt was so fond of. 'Did you look there?' he asked me. *'While you were searching the body?'* "

Ellery flung aside a cigaret he had never lit. "That question of his was what I finally remembered."

"He knew she was wearing the pendant . . ."

"Exactly, when no one could have known except ourselves—when we found her—and whoever had murdered her there five days earlier."

He sank deeper into his coat. "It was a blow, but there it was—John Carroll had murdered Felicia Hunt. He'd had the opportunity, of course. You and Velie agreed that the latest she could have been murdered was the preceding Sunday. That Sunday Carroll was still free on bail. It wasn't until the next morning, Monday, you'll recall, that he had to resubmit to the custody of the court for the commencement of his trial."

"But it doesn't add up," Inspector Queen spluttered. "The Hunt woman's testimony could get him an acquittal. Why should Carroll have knocked off the only witness who could give him his alibi?"

"Just what I asked myself. And the only answer that made sense was: Carroll must have had reason to believe that when Felicia took the stand in court, she was going to tell the truth."

"Truth? About what?"

"About Carroll's alibi being false."

"False?"

"Yes. And from his standpoint, of course, that would compel him to shut her mouth. To protect the alibi."

"But without her he had no alibi, true *or* false!"

"Correct," Ellery said softly, *"But when Carroll drove up to Westchester he didn't know that; at that time he thought he had her signed statement locked in his office safe*. He didn't learn until days after he had killed her—when West and I opened the safe and found the envelope empty—that he no longer had possession of the alibi statement, hadn't had possession for months, in fact—that, as I pointed out to him, Felicia Hunt must have lifted it from his briefcase while he was downstairs showing the notary out. No wonder he almost collapsed."

"I'll be damned," the Inspector said. "I'll be double-damned!"

Ellery shrugged. "If Carroll's alibi for Meredith Hunt's murder was a phony, then the whole case against him stood as charged. The alibi was the only thing that gave him the appearance of innocence. If in fact he had no alibi, everything pointed to his guilt of Hunt's murder, as the jury rightfully decided.

"Carroll filled in the details for me earlier tonight in the Death House." Ellery's glance went back to the wall. "He said that when he left his house that rainy night after Hunt's ultimatum, to walk off his anger, the fog gave him a slight lease on hope. Maybe Hunt's plane was grounded and Hunt was still within reach. He phoned La Guardia and found that all the flights had been delayed for a few hours. On the chance that Hunt was hanging around the airport, Carroll stopped in at his office and got his target pistol. He had some vague idea, he said, of threatening Hunt into a change of heart.

"He took a cab to La Guardia, found Hunt waiting for the fog to clear, and persuaded him to get his car from the parking lot so that they could talk in privacy. Eventually Hunt meandered back to Manhattan and parked on East 58th Street. The talk in the car became a violent quarrel. Carroll's hair-trigger temper went off, and he shot Hunt. He left Hunt in the Thunderbird and stumbled back home in the rain.

"The next morning, when we called on Mrs. Hunt to announce her husband's killing and found Carroll and West there, and you mentioned that the killer had left his gun in Hunt's car, Carroll was sick. Remember he ran into the bathroom to gag? He wasn't acting that time. For the first time he realized that, in his fury and panic, he'd completely forgotten about the gun.

"As a lawyer," Ellery droned on, "he knew what a powerful circumstantial case loomed against him, and that the only thing that could save him was an equally powerful alibi. He saw only one possible way to get it. He had never destroyed the love letters Felicia Hunt had written him during her infatuation. And he knew her dread of scandal. So he fabricated a statement out of the whole cloth about having spent the murder period in her bedroom 'pleading' with her to intercede with her husband, and he took the statement to her. He didn't have to spell out his threat. Felicia understood clearly enough the implication of his proposal . . . that if she didn't give him the phony alibi he needed, he would publish her hot letters and ruin her with her straight-laced Latin-American family and compatriots. She signed."

"But why didn't Carroll produce the alibi right away, Ellery? What was his point in holding it back?"

"The legal mind again. If he produced it during the investigation, even if it served to clear him, the case would still be open on the books and he might find himself back in it up to his ears at any time. But if he stood trial for Hunt's murder and *then* produced the fake alibi and was acquitted—he was safe from the law forever by the rule of double jeopardy. He couldn't be tried again for Hunt's killing after that even if the alibi should at some future date be exposed as a fake.

"He knew from the beginning," Ellery went on, "that Felicia Hunt was the weak spot in his plan. She was neurotic and female and he was afraid she might blow under pressure when he needed her most. As the trial approached, Carroll told me, he got more and more nervous about her. So the day before it was scheduled to start, he decided to talk to her again. Learning that she'd gone into retreat up in Westchester, he found an excuse to get away from his family and drove up to the cottage. His worst fears were realized. She told him that she had changed her mind. Scandal or no scandal, she wasn't going to testify falsely under oath and lay herself open to perjury. What she didn't tell him—it might possibly have saved her life if she had—was that she's stolen and destroyed the alibi statement he had forced her to sign months before.

"Carroll grabbed the nearest heavy object and hit her over the head with it. Now at least, he consoled himself, she wouldn't be able to repudiate her signed statement, which he thought was in his office safe."

"And you've kept all this to yourself," his father muttered. "Why, Ellery? You certainly didn't owe Carroll anything."

Ellery turned form the wall. He looked desperately tired. "No, I didn't owe Carroll anything . . . a man with a completely cockeyed moral sense . . . too proud to live on his wife's money, yet capable of stealing twenty thousand dollars . . . a faithful husband who nevertheless kept the love letters of a woman he despised for their possible future value to him . . . a man with a strange streak of honesty who was also capable of playing a scene like an actor. . . a loving father who permitted himself to murder two people.

"No, I didn't owe him anything," Ellery said, "but he wasn't the only one involved. And no one knew that better than Carroll. The afternoon that the answer came to me, while we were waiting for the jury to come in, I told Mrs. Carroll I couldn't save her husband, that it was too late. Carroll was the only one present who knew what I meant. He knew I meant it was too late for *him*, that I couldn't save him because I knew he was guilty. And when I put it up to him, he made me understand that I wasn't to give him away. It wasn't for his own sake—he knew the verdict the jury was going to bring in. He knew he was already a dead man.

"And so I respected his last request. I couldn't save him, but I could save his family's memories of him. This way Helena Carroll and little Breck and Louanne will always think John Carroll died the victim of a miscarriage of justice." Ellery shucked his topcoat and headed for his bedroom. "How could I deny them that comfort?"

About the Author

The team of FREDERIC DANNAY and MANFRED B. LEE—who, as everyone knows, are Ellery Queen—has written 53 books, including those first published under the pseudo-pseudonym of Barnaby Ross, and has edited 52 more. A conservative estimate has placed their total sales in various editions at more than 70,000,000 copies. And millions of listeners agreed when *TV Guide* awarded the Ellery Queen program its National Award as the best mystery show of 1950. Ellery Queen has won five annual "Edgars" (the national Mystery Writers of America awards similar to the "Oscars" of Hollywood), including the Grand Master award of 1960, and both the silver and gold "Gertrudes" awarded by Pocket Books.

Ellery Queen's most recent successes are *And On the Eighth Day* and *The Player on the Other Side*. He is internationally known as an editor—*Ellery Queen's Mystery Magazine* celebrated its twenty-fourth anniversary in 1965. His library of first editions (which is now at the University of Texas) contained the finest collection of books and manuscripts of detective short stories in the world. These facts about Queen may account for the remark by Anthony Boucher, in his profile of Manfred B. Lee and Frederic Dannay, that "Ellery Queen *is* the American detective story."

MIND-BOGGLING MYSTERIES
from
🅱🅱
BALLANTINE BOOKS

AND ON THE EIGHTH DAY
Ellery Queen $1.25

ONE-MAN SHOW Michael Innes $1.25

THE BIG SLEEP Raymond Chandler $1.50

INSPECTOR QUEEN'S OWN CASE
Ellery Queen $1.50

EIGHTY MILLION EYES Ed McBain $1.25

FAREWELL, MY LOVELY
Raymond Chandler $1.50

CAT OF MANY TAILS Ellery Queen $1.50

SILENCE OBSERVED Michael Innes $1.25

▼ Available at your local bookstore or mail the coupon below ▼

BB 63/75